T0197864

**If Harper was telling
Animal Shelter migh
her out.**

But if she'd staged all of this to give her access to
research a story?

"You wouldn't write any articles about it?" Scott
demanded.

"Not about that aspect of it, and only if it made sense
to write something about the rescued animals."

In other words, Scott wasn't ready to trust Harper.

Was Bryson?

But if Harper actually was telling the truth...

"Tell you what," Bryson said. "How about if Harper
moves in with me for now? I have a spare bedroom
in my apartment, and she could help us here at Barky
Boulevard while I keep an eye out for anyone after
her. And in case you're wondering, Harper, I have no
intention of trying to restart the relationship we had
before. I'd just like to make sure you and the rescue
facility are both as safe as possible."

"Great idea," Scott said.

"Thanks, Bryson," Harper said hoarsely...and it hurt
him to see the tears running down her face.

What did she really think?

And were she and her story for real?

Dear Reader,

Canine Protection is the fourth book in my Shelter of Secrets series for Harlequin Romantic Suspense. As with the others in this series, it takes place at the very special Chance Animal Shelter and the nearby town of Chance, California.

In it, Harper Morsley, a popular writer of feature articles in multiple publications, all involving animals, has had her life threatened. Her research has told her about the highly covert Chance Animal Shelter, which protects people in trouble as well as animals. She needs to be accepted there for her safety but knows she will not be able to write about it for the sake of the residents. On her arrival in town with her dog, Lorrie, she's shocked to find her former lover, Bryson Crague, living in Chance, though not at the shelter. And when she isn't immediately welcomed into the shelter because of concern over her telling the world what it's really about, cop on leave Bryson takes on her protection, at least until she's accepted. Their relationship is long over—but the attraction is stirred up again by their nearness. Will Harper survive? And will Bryson remain in her life this time?

I hope you enjoy *Canine Protection*. Please come visit me at my website, www.lindaojohnston.com, and at my weekly blog, www.killerhobbies.blogspot.com. And, yes, I'm on Facebook and Writerspace, too.

Linda O. Johnston

CANINE PROTECTION

LINDA O. JOHNSTON

Harlequin

ROMANTIC SUSPENSE

If you purchased this book without a cover you should be aware that this book is stolen property. It was reported as "unsold and destroyed" to the publisher, and neither the author nor the publisher has received any payment for this "stripped book."

Harlequin®
ROMANTIC SUSPENSE™

Recycling programs for this product may not exist in your area.

ISBN-13: 978-1-335-50248-3

Canine Protection

Copyright © 2024 by Linda O. Johnston

All rights reserved. No part of this book may be used or reproduced in any manner whatsoever without written permission.

Without limiting the author's and publisher's exclusive rights, any unauthorized use of this publication to train generative artificial intelligence (AI) technologies is expressly prohibited.

This is a work of fiction. Names, characters, places and incidents are either the product of the author's imagination or are used fictitiously. Any resemblance to actual persons, living or dead, businesses, companies, events or locales is entirely coincidental.

For questions and comments about the quality of this book, please contact us at CustomerService@Harlequin.com.

TM and ® are trademarks of Harlequin Enterprises ULC.

Harlequin Enterprises ULC
22 Adelaide St. West, 41st Floor
Toronto, Ontario M5H 4E3, Canada
www.Harlequin.com

Printed in U.S.A.

Linda O. Johnston loves to write. While honing her writing skills, she worked in advertising and public relations, then became a lawyer...and enjoyed writing contracts. Linda's first published fiction appeared in *Ellery Queen's Mystery Magazine* and won a Robert L. Fish Memorial Award for Best First Mystery Short Story of the Year. Linda now spends most of her time creating memorable tales of romantic suspense, paranormal romance and mystery. Visit www.lindaojohnston.com.

Books by Linda O. Johnston

Harlequin Romantic Suspense

Shelter of Secrets

Her Undercover Refuge
Guardian K-9 on Call
Undercover Cowboy Defender
Canine Protection

K-9 Ranch Rescue

Second Chance Soldier
Trained to Protect

The Coltons of Colorado

Shielding Colton's Witness

The Coltons of New York

CSI Colton and the Witness

Visit the Author Profile page
at Harlequin.com for more titles.

Once again, many thanks to my wonderful editor, Allison Lyons, and my fantastic agent, Paige Wheeler.

Like the other books in the Shelter of Secrets series, *Canine Protection* is dedicated to the wonderful people who devote their lives to helping other people in trouble, and also to those who work for and volunteer at shelters where dogs, cats and other animals without human families are cared for.

And, as I always do, I dedicate this book to my dear husband, Fred, as well as our delightful, loving dogs, Cari and Roxie.

Chapter 1

With her black French bulldog, Lorrie, leashed beside her, Harper Morsley strode through the glass door at the front of Barky Boulevard, the doggy day care center in the middle of the town of Chance, California, amused at the loudness of the dogs and people playing games there.

Oh, yes, she strode in with Lorrie, hoping to present her usual confident air as a prominent and popular journalist showing up to interview people for her next article on animals—usually pet rescues or pet-sitters, but also wildlife or any other ideas she had that her vast readership might like. She wore an attractive beige knit shirt, clingy dark pants and slight heels that were easy to walk in.

Perky, strong and on top of the world was the image she intended to present.

Even now, when her world was falling apart.

She entered a large room, with mats on the floor and small wood-slatted enclosures along the walls. Those walls were light blue—maybe so the color could be seen by dogs, whose ability to see colors was limited.

And, yes, dogs were present, lots of them on the floor throughout the room, playing with each other and a few people who teased them with toys. Dogs of all sizes and backgrounds, from Chihuahuas to German shepherd mixes. A few were barking or jumping as the people called out to them. They all appeared to be having fun. And Lorrie, in a halter so she wouldn't get choked, pulled a bit on her leash, clearly wanting to join in.

"Sit," Harper said, and happy about it or not, Lorrie obeyed. Not surprising. Her beloved pup was smart. She was also obedient, partly because Harper had learned a lot about animal training in her career.

Harper smiled, and her mind began making notes as it always did in locations where dogs were being cared for in one way or another. But she stood beside Lorrie and just watched for now, even as a couple of the people sitting on the floor—a teen and a grinning lady—glanced at her. Harper wasn't here to research a story, not exactly, although she couldn't help hoping one would evolve from this situation. Maybe more than one.

But if things were as she suspected around here, she would have to be damn careful about what she said and how she said it.

And even more...well, she was here because she didn't just want to write a story.

She wanted to save her own life.

But this wasn't the place she thought she needed to go. She'd been told to come here though, to start the process, whatever it might be, and to meet Scott Sherridan, the director of the Chance Animal Shelter. The shelter was located near the edge of town from what Harper had determined.

He was going to interview her. Which seemed offbeat.

She was used to interviewing other people for her articles, not the other way around.

But Scott wasn't going to write about her. From what she understood, he would decide if she could become a resident, temporary or otherwise, at the shelter.

She couldn't help hoping for that outcome at the moment, if her assumption was correct, and the shelter took in people in danger to keep them safe, without letting the world know their location, and what the shelter was really about.

She didn't see anyone who might be Scott, although she wasn't certain what he looked like. She had definitely done her usual thing of conducting research on the Chance Animal Shelter, her initial goal, but as far as she could tell, Scott didn't have anything to do with Barky Boulevard. And the online info on this doggy day care site was a bit limited, even though the few reviews raved about the day care and all it did to take care of pups being dog-sat. Not much about the people connected with it though, except that the owner's name was Andrea.

And the reports on Chance Animal Shelter, were limited too, which didn't surprise her, although a few social media posts showed pets cared for there who'd found new forever homes. But she hadn't seen any pictures of Scott.

There weren't any men in the room older than maybe their early twenties, and she figured Scott, with his responsibilities, was most likely older.

So where was he?

As she scanned the room, she saw an older woman at the far side rise from where she'd been kneeling to do a tug-of-war with what appeared to be a border collie mix. The woman walked in Harper's direction.

"Can I help you?" she asked, glancing down at Lorrie, then back up into Harper's face.

"Oh, I'm supposed to meet someone here," Harper said. She noticed that a door at the far side of the room had started opening, and a moment later, a man walked out.

"Are you meeting Scott here?" the woman asked.

"That's right." Harper wondered what she'd been told. What anyone had been told. This meeting was supposed to be confidential. But still, it was in a public place so it wasn't surprising staff had been told she was expected.

"Harper?" the man asked as he maneuvered toward her through the mélange of dogs and people. He was tall and wore a gray sweatshirt over jeans, and was fairly good-looking. With his background and appearance, she had an urge to interview him—which was ridiculous under the circumstances, regardless of his experience saving animals.

Not now, at least.

"Yes, that's me." She smiled. "Are you Scott Sherridan?"

"That's right. Why don't you come this way? We can talk in the office." He gestured toward the door he had just exited, then began walking back to it.

"Of course." Harper weaved through the crowd along with Lorrie, who tried to stop and trade nose sniffs with a few dogs, mostly larger ones. "Come, Lorrie," Harper said, and once more her pup obeyed. Harper continued toward that door, but even as Lorrie traded more nose sniffs, Harper couldn't help stooping now and then to pat the heads of some of those dogs. Heck, she loved animals, especially dogs. That was why she'd embarked on the career she had. The career she loved.

The career that had somehow gotten her into trouble, and she didn't know how or why.

Well, she needed to step back and take care of herself right now, and Scott Sherridan just might have the best way for her to do that.

As she got closer to him, he gestured for her to enter that doorway first, but she and Lorrie were still working their way through the nearby dogs. He smiled as she walked past with her pup and entered the next room, which appeared to be a regular office, with a large desk and several chairs, as well as photos of dogs on the walls.

But those photos weren't what stopped Harper from continuing on.

The man in the room did.

She gasped as she saw him. She wasn't expecting to see him here—or anywhere, for that matter.

Bryson Crague stood near the desk, watching her.

Bryson, the man she had once thought she'd loved.

Why was he here? She knew he cared for animals too. But why did the LA cop happen to be in this doggy day care center, in this town, where she'd needed to come possibly to save her life?

"Hi, Harper," he said. Oh, yes, it was Bryson, as if she'd doubted it. But she definitely recognized that deep, sexy voice she hadn't heard in years. "So what's really going on with you?"

He didn't exactly sound friendly. But he might be friends with Scott, maybe even associated with the shelter she was here to learn about—and to hopefully do more than visit.

He looked the same as she remembered—oh, so well. Tall, broad-shouldered, utterly handsome with his dark hair, including a hint of facial hair. Wearing a muted blue plaid shirt over jeans.

How should she handle this?

"Hi, Bryson," she said carefully, drawing closer and holding out her hand for a shake as if they were business associates, or someone she was hoping to interview for a story.

But who was he now? At the moment, she wasn't really working on one of her articles.

He'd asked her a question though. Was he attempting to interview her? Ha! But she decided to respond.

He reached out and shook her hand. It felt strange—and good—to feel his warm, hard grip. She started to recall what it felt like to have that hand elsewhere…and threw that thought out of her mind.

"What's really going on with me?" She searched his deep brown eyes, trying to see what was actually inside his head. "Oh, not much different from when you knew me. I'm still writing a lot of stories featuring animals for a lot of publications, print and online and wherever. How about you?"

She wondered what he thought, seeing her. Oh, she didn't think she'd changed much in the past three years—had it been that long? She still had wavy blond hair. And her face? Well, not gorgeous but not bad-looking either, she believed, and she added makeup in a way she thought was attractive, or hoped so. She was far from being a model, but she wanted to look as good as possible since photos of her were often used at the end of her stories, to show who had written them. No, she wasn't as appealing as the animals who were the subjects of her articles, but she wanted to enhance how they were featured.

"And you're writing a story about the Chance Animal Shelter?" Bryson's tone sounded demanding and maybe a bit angry.

But before she could respond, intending to reassure Scott that wasn't what she had in mind—not now, at least—Scott intervened.

"Harper and I need to talk," he said, looking at Bryson. "Maybe someday she'll write a story about our animal rescues, but right now we're going to discuss some things going on in Harper's life to determine if she can visit the shelter in another capacity for a while."

"That's what I understand." Bryson's tone sounded a bit more cordial. "But I want to be sure Harper understands that she can't just—"

"Assuming the shelter is what I think it is," she interrupted, "there's no way I'll disclose that to the world. And if I can get some help there—"

"Let's talk about what's going on in your life now," Scott said, "and see if we can be of some help." He had shifted closer to Bryson. They remained near the now-closed door. "If we can hang out here in your office, Bryson, we can discuss it—assuming you're okay with Bryson hearing too, Harper. But since you two know each other, maybe he can help."

Harper doubted it. But she suspected if she made a fuss, made it clear she didn't really want the man she'd been so attracted to once to hear how her life had taken a bad turn, that might make it more difficult for her to get Scott's approval.

If the shelter was the kind of place she thought, she could use some time there to reorganize her life. Feel safe, at least for a while.

But this was Bryson's office? Things must have changed a lot in his life. Maybe she would hear what had happened.

She said, "Sure, that would be fine with me." She made herself smile at Bryson. "It's always good to talk to old friends again."

She hoped.

Okay, he'd known she was coming.

At first Scott had just asked if it was okay if he interviewed a possible new resident, a potential "staff member" at the Chance Animal Shelter, somewhere secluded at Barky Boulevard. He'd said the person might need some protection at the moment, but because of her career in the public eye, he didn't want to conduct his first interview at his shelter, with its highly secret underlying purpose. He wanted to feel certain the meeting with his interviewee would be as discreet as necessary.

And Bryson guessed almost immediately who that interviewee was when Scott indicated she had a career in the public eye as a well-known, popular journalist who wrote mostly articles about animals.

Harper Morsley.

And here she was, beautiful as ever. As well-known and popular for her broad-reaching articles on animals and animal protection as Scott had indicated.

But why was she in danger? He forced his breathing to slow. Shouldn't give a damn, but he did. A lot.

He wanted to hear what was going on in her life. And would he be able to help protect her?

It wasn't really his business, not anymore. But if someone was after her, wanting to hurt her—or worse—

he wanted to know. And if he could do anything about it…? His fists clenched, but he made his hands relax.

Scott asked Harper to sit on one of the chairs at the side of the room. "Would you like anything to drink?" he asked her. "Water or coffee?"

"No, but thank you." Her gaze toward the shelter director did seem grateful…and pleading. And Bryson again had an urge to get closer and even hug her.

Scott sat beside her. Bryson wanted to stand by the door and observe but figured that might appear too remote, or even critical, so he instead took a seat at Scott's other side. Fortunately, the row of seats was a bit uneven, allowing him to watch Harper's face. She blinked her beautiful green eyes, looked directly at Scott, then down again.

But then she straightened her posture, once more the smart, determined journalist he knew her to be. "I assume you want to hear why I would like to spend some time at Chance Animal Shelter, assuming it's the kind of place I've heard it is."

"Where did you hear it?" Scott asked sharply. "And from whom?"

Harper closed her eyes briefly and looked down. "As I told you when I first contacted you, I interview a lot of people so I can write stories about animals. I happened to be conducting one of those interviews at the Care Forever Animal Shelter in Ventura, California, when…well, I received one of the threats I'll tell you about. I guess… I guess the horror I suddenly felt must have been obvious, since one of the security personnel there that I knew asked what was wrong. I told him a little about it, and he was kind enough to let me know he'd heard a secret—a place I might want to go check out, a different animal shelter that is covertly reputed to be a shelter for people in danger too. I did some research before contacting you and only learned that you hire some homeless people to help with the animals you take in. But— Well, I figured it wouldn't hurt to get in touch with you and ask more about the Chance Animal Shelter and… I guess what I said might have made sense to you, Scott, since you invited me to come here and talk."

Bryson tensed. What kind of threats had she been getting? From whom? Bryson wanted to learn more, a lot more, and go after whoever had scared her.

Although— Was she really scared? He hadn't talked to Harper for a long time. Was this some kind of ploy on her part to learn more about the shelter after hearing rumors about it?

He would protect the Chance Animal Shelter from danger too. That was more his responsibility now…kind of. He was currently a resident of Chance, after all. And an animal aficionado. A friend of Scott's as well as a volunteer at the shelter—and someone who truly cared about animals and people in danger.

Like those the shelter took in.

And like Harper?

"Okay, then," Scott said gently. "Tell us about those threats."

Bryson watched Harper closely. Her eyes welled up, and she bit her lower lip before speaking. Sure, she could be a good actress. But her distress looked real, raising his urge to get close and hug her.

Instead, he just listened, and glanced at Scott, who listened too.

"I… Well, I write freelance for a lot of publications, both online and in print, but primarily for three magazines— *Pup Rescue Forever, Puppies, Kittens and Humans*, and *Pets and Love*. Over the past couple of months, each time I had an article published in each magazine I've received some good reviews and some nasty ones, which is not unusual. And also recently I've received at least half a dozen emails that trash what I've written and say something like the person sending them knows where I live and intends to come there and hurt me, or more, if I don't stop writing my trash. Soon. Lately they've been a lot worse. They've threatened my dog too." She glanced down and patted her little companion on the head. The pup looked up at her and seemed to sense her fear, since she stood and licked her owner's hand.

Harper smiled briefly at that, as Scott said, "Could you tell who it was, where the emails came from, or anything?"

"Not at all. The name used in those emails was always something like Angry Reader, and they used a general email address."

"Show one to us," Bryson said. What was this all about?

Was Harper really in trouble? It certainly didn't sound good, but she was creative. If she made this up…but why would she?

"Here's the most recent, worst one," she said. "The one I was looking at when the security guy suggested I look into this shelter." She brought it up on her phone's email link and showed it first to Scott, then Bryson.

It took a short while for them each to read it, and

what it said caused both men to sit up straighter. Bryson couldn't help growling. "Damn."

It was critical, and particularly nasty. It ended, "Your dear articles are mostly cute but not real. You're not trustworthy. And so, if you don't stop writing, you will be killed. Soon. Like an animal. And in case you're wondering, I know where you live. I've even visited nearby. Watch for me." Bryson glanced at Harper after he finished reading it and saw that Scott had too. Harper's smile was forced and it was obvious she'd tried to remain calm as the men read it.

"Any idea who sent it?" Scott demanded.

"No. I googled it, as well as all the others as they came in, but couldn't find anything. I even showed some a while back to a cop at a local police station, who told me they couldn't do anything when it's just online harassment. They told me to check with an online private investigator, but all I could find were expensive sources who didn't seem to suggest anything helpful. Meanwhile, not only did I get those horrible emails but so did my editors, and we all saw some nasty critiques on social media and—" She hesitated, then continued, "Fortunately, I'm the only one being threatened, or they all might stop buying my stories. But they're always asking me if I've seen the nasty reviews online and telling me that maybe I'd better stop writing." Her voice cracked a bit, but Bryson made himself remain seated.

"Anyway, I first saw the message I just showed you a couple of days ago in Ventura when I returned to my car in a parking lot after interviewing someone at Care Forever for an article. I obviously reacted, since that security guy I mentioned saw how upset I was and asked what was going on. I didn't tell him much, but enough that he suggested I look into Chance Animal Shelter, in case it was what he'd secretly heard about." She looked intensely at Scott. "Is it?"

"What did he tell you?" Scott countered.

"That your facility, though it's reputed to hire homeless people to help care for the rescued animals, also rescues people in trouble."

Bryson knew that was true. And if Harper was telling the truth, Chance Animal Shelter might be perfect to help her out.

But if she'd staged all of this to give her access to research a story? Bryson assumed that's what Scott was wondering...and he couldn't help wondering too.

It certainly seemed extreme.

"And if it were that kind of facility, you wouldn't write any articles about it?" Scott demanded.

"Not about that aspect of it, and only if it made sense to write something about the rescued animals."

Scott nodded. "I appreciate that." He seemed to hesitate. "But whether or not it's what you believe, I've been looking into your stories and I'm just not sure if you'd be right for our facility, even with those threatening emails that don't have an identified source."

In other words, Bryson figured, he wasn't ready to trust Harper.

Was Bryson? Could he be sure Harper hadn't faked that message and was just making claims about more? He really doubted she'd do something awful like that, even to help research a story.

Still, for the rescue facility's sake, Bryson would prefer more proof.

But if Harper actually was telling the truth…

"Tell you what," Bryson said. "How about if Harper moves in with me for now? I have a spare bedroom in my apartment, and she could help us here at Barky Boulevard while I keep an eye out for anyone after her. She could visit Chance Animal Shelter at first and maybe move in there later, depending on how things go. And in case you're wondering, Harper, I have no intention of trying to restart the relationship we had before. I'd just like to make sure you, and the rescue facility, are both as safe as possible."

"Great idea," Scott said. "Thanks, Bryson."

And then Bryson looked at Harper, waiting for her response.

"Thanks, Bryson," she said hoarsely…and it hurt him to see the tears running down her face.

What did she really think?

And were she and her story for real?

Chapter 2

Okay. That was enough, Harper told herself. Crying wasn't going to get her anywhere even if she wanted to let more tears flow, mostly in relief. And hope.

And she knew Lorrie was concerned, since her dear pup snuggled against her leg, again attempting to calm her.

She succeeded just a little, as Harper bent over to pat her.

But where was the brave journalist who'd strode in here just a short while ago with that wonderful dog?

She'd known what would be discussed. What danger in her life she would need to reveal.

But she hadn't known she would see Bryson here.

Or that he would step in to protect her when Scott Sherridan hadn't seemed ready to do so now, if he ever would.

Bryson, once a military officer, had been a cop three years ago. Was he now? It didn't appear that way, but what did she know about him anymore?

Not a lot, although he seemed to have something to do with this doggy day care facility and had always cared for animals.

She squared her shoulders as she remained in her

seat. "I wish I could tell you what you'd be getting into by letting me become your roommate, Bryson." Roommate? No, housemate or apartment-mate.

Roommate sounded much too intimate.

As things once had been between them…

"I can guess the possibilities," Bryson said before she could attempt to correct what she'd said. "It would certainly be more helpful if we knew who was issuing those threats. And whether they actually know where you live, and where you are now. But we'll just have to deal with all that. We'll figure it out." He looked at Scott. "And I'll do my damnedest to keep Harper safe right here."

If Harper read it right, Bryson was telling Scott it was okay for him to assume the worst to keep his facility safe. The worst about *her*. Well, somehow she would have to convince them both, maybe Bryson first, that she hadn't fabricated anything and wasn't trying to do anything to undermine the Chance Animal Shelter and those people being protected there.

Or publicize it, despite her beloved career as a feature-writing journalist.

People being protected there as she might be someday? Soon? Like, now?

She would prefer it if the threats would just stop and she could get back to her real life. She would do all she could while hanging out here or wherever, though, to keep on writing and selling her articles remotely, as she usually did. And she never really disclosed where she was, though staying silent about it hadn't been particularly important before.

And despite Bryson's kind, sweet, brave offer to watch over her, to try to keep her safe, and even with his background, could she rely on him even a fraction of how she'd be able to rely on the Chance Animal Shelter? From the little she'd heard here, and the lack of adamant denials of it being what she believed it was, she thought even more that the shelter helped people in trouble.

Like her.

But she had no doubt that, with Bryson's military and law-enforcement background and his intelligence, he would do a great job protecting her, on his own and right here in the middle of Chance rather than in a special facility. At least as best as he could by himself—with her assistance, as much as she was able to help.

Well, she didn't have a lot of choices, not if she wanted to stay as safe as possible. But she also would want to protect Bryson as much as possible too if whoever was after her learned someone was helping her and went after him as well.

The two men had gotten into a conversation as she pondered what to say next. Bryson, clearly in charge, described how pets were accepted at Barky Boulevard for day care. The owners didn't have to do a lot to get their dogs to qualify, just bring them in and show they weren't aggressive and had received some basic training.

That didn't indicate much screening, much ability to ensure that the customers weren't nasty and threatening.

Would Scott buy in to that, and realize Bryson, despite his background, might not be able to keep her safe? Did he believe she needed to be kept safe?

Well, for now, at least, Harper would have to deal with the situation. Under Bryson's protection, but also using her own skills to take care of herself, and make sure Bryson's facility, and his employees and the pets they cared for, remained safe.

She didn't want to be the cause of any turmoil. But could she avoid it?

Heck, yes. She had to.

But how? Well, by not letting anyone know where she was, of course. Yet since she didn't know who was threatening her, where they might be…

She needed to join the discussion. "Okay, here's how I see things, at least for now," she said when there was a slight lull. "Bryson, I'll kind of go undercover here. In writing my stories, I occasionally do that, so it won't be obvious who I am and why I'm at a particular facility researching a story, when that facility is at least a bit controversial in its treatment of pets. I may use a pseudonym I've come up with in the past. I've already shut off the GPS in my cell phone." She had started keeping it off a lot of the time since the threats had begun. "And hopefully I'll be of some use here helping with your canine customers." Hoping she would learn about why he was here running this place now, she once more bent and patted Lorrie. "Meantime, we'll both keep our eyes open for anyone who comes in who seems difficult." She sucked in her bottom lip for a moment. "And I'll continue to check my social media accounts and emails to watch for more threats."

"Will you stay in touch with those editors who are aware of those threats?" Scott asked.

"Yes," she said immediately.

But at the same time, Bryson said, "No."

She turned and looked at him, frowning. "But I need

to know what's going on in the rest of the world if it affects me."

"While you're doing this, while you're in downtown Chance, at least, you need to be silent to the rest of the world."

She fought the urge to stand and put her hands on her hips as she contradicted Bryson loudly. But she continued sitting and spoke softly instead.

"I may take on another name to the world around me," she said. "But I need to continue in some ways to be me, not only to earn a living but to keep up my career. I've already researched a few stories I can write and submit remotely, maybe to different media or publications. But even if Harper Morsley goes quiet as a person, she needs to continue as an out-there journalist."

To her surprise, Bryson laughed. "Yes, I guess you are an out-there person. And even if you are suddenly here as a Barky Boulevard employee, that doesn't mean you can't be both…as long as we're both careful about it."

We're both. She liked the sound of that. He seemed to be accepting what she'd said.

"All of this sounds good to me," Scott said. "I'll want you to stay in touch, especially if any of those threats occur. And, Harper, or whoever you become, please keep me informed about the articles you're writing and where they're being published. I'll do my own research too, to be sure you're honest with me. And if things go well with that and I feel the shelter will remain safe—but you actually are under threat as you showed us—then maybe my position on that will change. Okay?"

She wanted to confront Scott now, let him know she felt anger toward him for not trusting her and believing that email was genuine. For wanting to watch her remotely before deciding she was who she said and wasn't just here to endanger his shelter, and all its residents who were in trouble—assuming again that she understood what it was about—by her journalistic determination.

On the other hand, she could understand his wanting to protect those residents and be certain that another potential resident wasn't about to harm them.

"Okay," she said to him.

Then Bryson spoke to Scott. "I understand what you're doing," he said. "And in your position I'd probably do it too." He glanced toward Harper as if wanting to see her reaction. She attempted to appear neutral but wondered why Bryson was trying to help her when he seemed to be more on Scott's side. Still, he turned to her fully. "But even so, you don't have to worry. Maybe someday you can go stay at the shelter. But for now, you'll still be safe. Here, in Chance."

With me, she heard him say without saying it.

And oh, yes, despite what she believed about his underlying feelings, she felt all warm and fuzzy, and protected, inside. Whatever he'd decided with regard to her motives, he was taking control of protecting her.

And quite possibly keeping a close eye on her to make sure she wasn't planning anything nefarious.

Okay. She'd prove she was legit. And even with those emotions welling within her, Harper felt a bit worried a short while later when Scott said goodbye.

"But let's definitely keep in touch," he said as he reached the door in Bryson's office. "I'll make sure I don't sense any threats to the shelter, and you can both keep me informed about how things are going here and online at her publishing sources. If all goes well, it'll be time for Harper to visit the shelter, maybe one of the times you come up there to help, Bryson." And then he left.

No reason to feel so abandoned, Harper thought. Especially with Bryson here, taking her in, at least temporarily, for her protection. And probably observing her.

But from what she understood, she'd be able to feel pretty safe at the shelter.

Here too? Well, she did trust Bryson, despite her suspicions of how he wasn't just watching her to protect her, but also to protect the shelter from her doing something nasty to reveal it to the world, which she wouldn't do. He apparently did help some at the shelter, after all.

Would what had happened between them before be a factor? If so, it probably wouldn't be to her benefit.

And she'd have to remain alert even if Scott accepted her at his facility. She'd just have to be even more alert here, staying in town rather than in hiding. And try to convince Bryson she wasn't attempting to harm anyone or any facility by writing her stories—she just wanted to maintain her career. And protect herself.

She wasn't the kind of person who liked to hide, anyway. And here, she might be able to research an article about the town of Chance, and Barky Boulevard, for a future story even as she continued to go online and get information about other places, people and animals she might want to write about, while keeping her location a secret and not disclosing anything she shouldn't.

"So what are you thinking?" Bryson asked. He was no longer sitting beside her, but had moved behind the desk in the room.

Presumably his desk.

At his question, she squared her shoulders yet again and made herself smile at him. "Hey, I'm thinking I want you to teach me how you like best to take care of and play with the dogs in your care here. Looks like I'll be here for a while, and I might as well make myself useful."

And she meant that, even though she had no intention of stopping her researching and writing, and submitting stories to get published, in whatever way needed.

The thing was, Bryson thought, he had invited Harper to stay with him partly to protect her, but also to make sure she was telling the truth and didn't intend to do anything to jeopardize the underlying purpose of the Chance Animal Shelter—like make it public and endanger the people called "staff members" there, those under the shelter's protection.

He was all for how Scott had handled the situation, even if he'd now potentially put himself in a difficult position. But that was okay. Bryson wasn't in charge of those people in danger.

He was only in charge of protecting Harper.

Maybe.

For now…well, she'd asked to learn more about his doggy day care facility.

His? Well, partly his, since he'd stepped in and bought out half of his aunt Andrea's interest in it a year ago, when he'd learned she and her facility were in big financial trouble.

"Sure," Bryson now replied to Harper. "Why don't Lorrie and you come on out to the play area, and we'll all play a bit with our visitors for the day."

And he could watch this lovely woman play not only with her own pup, but also with others.

Which wouldn't really tell him what was on her mind, and how she intended to write any stories about this area.

Or do anything to harm the shelter and its occupants.

And damn if he didn't want her to be genuine now, he thought as he bent down to pat little Lorrie on the head, then straightened to guide both of his visitors back into the large play area.

Not that he liked the idea of that threat being real.

He stopped as he reached the office door though. Harper was right behind him.

"I want to introduce you to the people connected with this place," he told her, looking right into her pretty green eyes. "But you indicated you were going to take on a new persona. How should I introduce you?"

"Just call me Hanna," she told him. "I've used it as part of a pseudonym."

"Sounds good to me." He waved his arm to invite her to leave the office in front of him, and she and her dog were soon in the large play area.

He knew whom he wanted to introduce her to first, since at least for now she would be acting like an employee—so he could watch her and make sure she was okay, even as he conducted his usual business of greeting dogs who would hang out for doggy day care, as well as their owners.

And now he'd be even more alert, especially regarding anyone entering whom he hadn't met yet.

"Come on over here," he told Harper. He started walking toward where his aunt Andrea was kneeling on the floor playing tug-of-war with a long, braided toy with Scout, a smart, energetic border collie mix who came in nearly all weekdays.

"Oh, glad you found Scott, and also Bryson," Andrea said to Harper as she stood, still holding the toy. They'd spoken before, then?

"Thanks to you I did," Harper responded.

"Then I don't have to introduce you to my aunt," Bryson said to Harper, or "Hanna," half-teasing. He doubted she knew who Andrea was.

"Oh, it wouldn't hurt," Andrea said.

And so he did. "This is my aunt, Andrea Andell. Andrea and I are partners here at Barky," he added. He hadn't come here with Harper when they'd been dating, so she hadn't met all of his family members. Right now, he wasn't about to tell Harper why he'd become Andrea's partner, but that information might come out as they talked about this facility.

"Very nice to meet you," Harper said, holding out her hand as Andrea stood.

"Same here. Are you leaving your cute dog here for day care?" Andrea grinned eagerly, as she often did when they got a new client. She was in her late fifties, with long brown hair seasoned with gray streaks. She resembled her pretty sister, Bella, Bryson's mother, but wore a lot less makeup and perfume…maybe so she wouldn't bother the dogs with the additional aroma, although Bryson had never discussed that with either of them.

"Yes. Lorrie will be here," Bryson interjected. "But Hanna is a new employee. She's going to work with our clients. Maybe you can help her learn some of our rules and some of the more fun things we do." He also wasn't about to explain to his aunt what had brought Hanna here.

Or that he was going to make sure that she, and everyone else here, including the dogs, stayed safe.

He recognized that he would always think of her as Harper, but he would have to be careful to refer to her as Hanna here. Could he do it?

He had to.

Andrea shot him an inquisitive look, but she turned back to smile at Harper. "Sounds good. I'll be glad to help show you the ropes around here." She pulled up on the dog-toy rope she was holding and smiled.

"Thanks," Harper said. But just then a cell phone rang, probably hers since she appeared a bit startled as she reached into her purse. She looked at the screen and her eyes opened wider. "Sorry," she quickly said. "I have to get this."

She looked upset. Bryson hoped he would be able to eavesdrop. Was the person who'd been threatening her calling?

But he apparently wouldn't find out right away, since, holding Lorrie's leash, she hurried toward the side of the room with the phone held up to her ear.

Chapter 3

Harper hesitated but knew she had to answer the call despite her hand shaking. It was from Macie Smithston, editor in chief at *Puppies, Kittens and Humans* magazine, the publication she submitted articles to the most... and got them published.

It was also one of the publications where she'd been receiving criticisms and threats.

Making sure she was far enough away from Bryson and Andrea so they hopefully wouldn't be able to hear what she said, she told Lorrie to sit on the floor beside her. She kept her voice as low as possible despite noise from dogs and people as she faced the room's blue plaster wall near the office door, and, forced out a bright tone. "Hi, Macie. How are you?"

She hoped the editor was just fine and calling about a story idea, or asking the status of Harper's latest feature article. After all, Macie was ambitious and kind, and seemed to like Harper's stories a lot, always seeking more and encouraging her to sell her work to her publication.

But Harper couldn't help suspecting the worst.

And she was right.

"Hi, Harper. I've been better, and so have you." Fortunately, Harper was able to hear Macie despite the din around her. "I'm calling about something that just came in for you. Another email. Another threatening email."

"Then it's not *just* an email," Harper countered, trying to sound amused and upbeat but feeling the opposite. She'd always gotten the emails threatening her too, but hadn't seen anything on her phone recently. Her head lowered until her chin nearly touched her chest, and her heart rate soared, along with her short breaths. She spoke into her phone again. "So tell me about it."

"Okay, but you need to promise to come into the office within the next couple of days here in San Diego. Our publisher, Sally, received a similar kind of email that indicated your presence would alleviate some of the pressure."

Harper had met with the magazine's publisher, and Macie's boss, several times. Sally Effling was a nice lady, but always serious, and clearly determined to have the magazine keep climbing to the top of the successful publications lists.

But Harper didn't know what her own presence would do to help stop the emails, even if that was what they said. Unless the idea was that the sender wanted her to go there too, and…well, do something to her.

And concern about something like that was exactly why Harper had come here, hoping to stay far away from any place where that harasser would know how to find her. Stay under protection of the special shelter she had heard about, even if it should probably have remained more secret, though at least it had been someone in security who had suggested what it might be.

The Chance Animal Shelter—where she hadn't been accepted.

Not yet, at least.

But she wasn't willing to change her current plans, her current hopes, just because one of the editors she liked and respected, and wanted to continue to work with, had asked her to.

Especially because of the reason she'd asked Harper to come in for a visit.

"I get it," she replied to Macie. "And I wish I understood what was going on and could help. But I'm not near San Diego right now. And I'm in the middle of researching an article that requires my presence for a while, several weeks at least. I just can't leave and go to your office." She hesitated, but continued before Macie could respond, "We've received some strange correspondences there before and nothing came of them. I wish I understood what was going on, but hopefully it's just someone who wants publicity for some reason and is hoping to get it by harassing me, and you."

"But what if they're serious this time? I'd really like for you to come here so we can learn more. Maybe even tell the local authorities to send someone to check things out once you're here. And…well, I'd love for you to continue writing for us, but something like this certainly doesn't make us want to keep buying your material. And neither does that article in *Pup Rescue Forever* and the reviews and criticisms I've seen online for it."

What was Macie talking about? Stunned, Harper had to ask. "What article is that?" She attempted to keep her tone light.

"You haven't heard? It's your article about Pet Me For Life Shelter in Pasadena, the one published in *Pup Rescue Forever* a couple weeks ago. The people critiquing it say it's all wrong, contradictory to how that shelter really treats the animals it brings in—apparently far from being as caring as you described. The critiques specifically cite your article and mention you and claim everything you said is false, though it's not quite phrased that way."

"Oh, no," Harper breathed. "I visited there often, checked it out and did my research. I don't live too far from there so it was an easy place to check out and… Well, I didn't just rely on the good things the owners, staff and volunteers said. I don't understand what went wrong. And I didn't see any major criticisms when I checked out comments on social media."

"Well, I don't know either, and maybe some of the criticisms are just appearing. But, look. Why don't you come here to our offices? Just put the current article you're researching on hold for a while. We'll work on another article for *Puppies, Kittens and Humans* and give you full credit for it, and we'll help you restore your reputation, to the extent we can. Okay? When can we expect you here?"

Never, Harper wanted to scream.

And she had an urge to contact the other major publications she worked for most often. She'd received some additional threats before and minor criticisms. But the situation had been growing, becoming more menacing, forcing her here.

How bad was it? Was her reputation becoming totally ruined?

But if she visited all those publications, even contacted them to ask questions, her career could be harmed even more, right?

Well, she couldn't allow her panic to show. For now, she had to protect herself from those threats and not just worry about her career.

"I'm sorry, Macie, but I can't just drop the story I'm working on. I appreciate your offer to help, and I'll certainly keep it in mind when I'm finished with my research. But for now, I won't be able to come to your offices to look into this more."

Was she making a big mistake?

Or would it be a bigger one to do as Macie had suggested and get help from this editor and her major publication in person, at their offices?

Well, most important for now was that she physically survive.

And she felt she had the best possibility of doing that here, in Chance, especially if she could become a temporary resident at the Chance Animal Shelter.

And for now, to stay around Bryson, let him help with protecting her.

Bryson. Where was he? She'd remained in this same spot, staring at the wall, trying to hide what her expression must look like from the employees and others here she soon would be joining. No need for them to know her worries, her fear.

"I'll call you again soon, though, Macie," Harper said, trying to sound cheerful. "And thanks so much for letting me know what's going on and offering to help me."

"But—"

Harper didn't want to hear more. "'Bye now." She pushed the button to hang up and thrust her phone into her pocket.

She started to turn around and saw Lorrie rise on

the floor beside her and start wiggling her butt in an effort to wag the small corkscrew that was her French bulldog tail.

That's when Harper saw Bryson take a step toward them. He wasn't far away.

Had he been listening to her side of the call?

She looked at him and saw what appeared to be deep concern on his handsome face.

Bryson wished he'd been able to eavesdrop, but the noise around them, with cheerful people playing with and giving commands to barking pups, hadn't allowed him to hear Harper.

He'd moved nearer so he could see her face. Her expression suggested it hadn't been a good conversation. She appeared angry at times...but mostly afraid. He assumed he could still read her feelings, after all this time, and he believed he could.

And now that she'd ended the call, she still looked scared, but determined.

About what?

They had to talk. After all, he was now in charge of keeping her safe, but to do the best possible job, he had to know what was troubling her.

He drew even closer to her, pasting a smile on his face in case anyone was watching them. No one else needed to know Harper was upset.

No, *Hanna* was upset. He had to keep thinking of her that way when they were at Barky Boulevard, where she would soon start to work. Or appear to.

And her real identity needed to remain secret, at least for now. His aunt, their employees and others who came here with their dogs or to work with them were all involved in some way with caring for dogs. They probably also read articles in various publications about shelters and all where Harper's articles appeared—which he already knew about since he'd kind of kept track of her after their relationship ended. And she always had a byline as well as a picture. She still looked like herself, although her stress made her appear less like her glamorous photos.

No need for the others to know her true identity while she stayed here for protection.

But he remained proud of what she'd done with her life.

He had even missed her, appropriate or not, since he'd figured he would never see her again.

But now...

She kneeled down on the beige tiled floor, which was uneven to make it easier for the dogs to achieve traction and not slide while stopping from a run, and was hugging her own dog, appearing to play with the little French bull, but Bryson had the impression she was treating Lorrie like an emotional support dog.

Because Harper needed emotional support, even if Hanna didn't.

"Hey," he said, kneeling beside her. "I'd like to show you my condo, where you'll be staying." He kept his voice low, since he didn't want anyone around them to hear about that—although he recognized if the situation went on for any length of time, the employees might discover where Hanna was staying.

His aunt might figure it out too. And telling her it was not a relationship kind of situation, but one where he was attempting to keep his new roommate safe, might get awkward.

They'd probably need to pretend there was something between them. Something like what actually had been between them a while ago.

But for now, he wanted to show Harper the location of his condo and get her settled in. Fortunately, it was spacious and had a spare bedroom, so they could be there together yet stay apart.

And he definitely wanted to hear about the conversation she'd just had.

Harper had turned a bit to stare at him, seemingly to attempt to decipher his thoughts. Stay at his condo?

Yes, it would be better if he actually showed her how things were there.

"Okay," she told him softly. "But—"

"It'll be fine. You'll see. Are you parked near here? I assume you brought some clothes and other things since you planned to stay…near here for a while. Let's drive to my place and you can get unpacked." He paused, then added, "We can also discuss your phone call."

"Sounds like a good idea," she said in that same soft tone, then looked around perhaps to see if anyone was listening.

No one was particularly close.

"Great." He stood, then said more loudly, "Hey, let's take Lorrie for a walk before you start learning how to help out here, okay?"

He and his aunt and their employees mostly took their canine guests out back into a fenced-in area when they needed to go do their doggy things, but occasionally they took them on walks, so that shouldn't seem too offbeat.

On the other hand, with him going with Hanna and her dog, the others might assume faster than he hoped that there was something between them, more than one of the owners of this place helping one of their soon-to-be employees.

Well, they'd simply have to deal with that, whatever the timing was.

"Sounds good," Harper said, also standing.

Bryson walked through the crowd of people and pups, and told his aunt they'd be gone for a little while. Her smile seemed a bit wry as she looked from him to Hanna and back again. "We'll be fine here," she told him. "Have fun."

He wanted to say something to clarify that having fun wasn't in the equation, at least right now, but figured it best not to say anything.

And so, he soon led Harper, with Lorrie leashed beside her, out the day care center's front door.

The street in downtown Chance wasn't particularly busy at this time of day, midafternoon. The day care center was in an area that contained many kinds of stores, from a women's clothing shop to a hardware store, to a candy store.

They weren't far from the town's only pet store, or the local veterinary clinic, both appropriate to what went on here at doggy day care, though Bryson didn't visit either often. And he wasn't going to point them out to Harper unless she happened to be parked near one.

Their walk was short. Harper had left her car in an open lot down the street, where she'd had to pay.

He considered offering to pay the parking fee as she prepared to leave, with Lorrie strapped into the back seat, but figured that wouldn't be appropriate. He was kind of Harper's physical guardian at the moment, but that didn't mean he was her financial guardian as well.

He also considered offering to drive her car, a white SUV hybrid, but decided against that too. Nice, that she could afford a car like this as an independent journalist. He'd figured she was still successful, and this proved it.

But if she was taking on a new persona and not wanting to be recognized in this area, her license plate, at least, would need to be changed. As a former cop, Bryson had visited the local police station and been friendly with some of those there, including Police Chief Andrew Shermovski, known as Sherm. Sherm might be able to get a temporary plate for Harper.

And since Scott was an undercover cop, he might be able to help too.

Most of all, Bryson wanted to hear about the conversation she'd just had, but figured it could wait until neither of them was driving, and they had time to really talk.

And discuss it.

"So where are we heading?" she asked as she pulled out of the parking lot's driveway.

"Stop along the road here, and I'll give you the address to program into your GPS. I'll most likely be with you most of the time, at least for now, but it'll be good for you to be able to figure out how to get back and forth from my place to the day care center if you happen to be alone."

She shot him a look that suggested she was trying to figure out the details of what would be happening between them for the next few days. Well, so was he. But he wanted to do all he could to ensure her safety, without appearing too controlling.

Unless that turned out to be the best way to take care of her. He would just have to see.

She did as he said, and he gave her the address of the condo in the small development just outside town. He'd bought the condo a few months ago when he had moved here to help Aunt Andrea after his purchase of half her store hadn't helped her enough. She had her own home not too far from his development, but she'd bought it a while back before she'd started to lose money on the doggy day care.

Now that Bryson was here, they'd raised the day care rates just a bit and started providing additional programs for the dogs and their owners, such as training sessions, that cost extra.

And made the place more profitable again.

Harper programmed his address, Fortune Lane, into her GPS. The streets in his development were named for luck…and Chance, including Kismet Street and Fate Boulevard. He found it amusing, but had chosen his place because of its nearby location and reasonable price considering where it was and its size.

She drove them there at a moderate speed, and at the gate Bryson told her what code number to press into the entry pad. He had a remote control in his car, and would get her one too, depending on how long she would be staying.

He directed her once more along the residential streets lined with nice, relatively new buildings. Soon, they arrived in front of his building.

"This is it," he said. "Just head down that driveway

and park, and then we'll start getting your things out of the car."

She did as he instructed and parked in a space behind the building. When they got out of the car though, she said, "I'd like to see how things are before I start bringing things in."

He wasn't surprised, considering who Harper was and how she liked to be in control, but reminded her, "And if you don't like it, where will you go?"

She stared at him over the hood. He kept his expression bland…and she caved first. "You're right," she said. "Let's get my stuff out, and I'll follow you."

She didn't appear happy, but at least she was still smart as always.

And the first thing she did when she got out of the car was leash Lorrie.

Chapter 4

Before getting anything else out of her car, Harper walked Lorrie around the edge of the parking lot, partly so the pup could do what she needed, but also to allow Harper to get her bearings.

She was about to enter the place where she would be staying, and for who knew how long… And living with Bryson.

She glanced up at the building. It looked identical to those on either side of it in this nice Chance development. All were six stories high, with large windows that indicated perhaps six units were on each of the floors.

It was an attractive structure and she wasn't surprised that Bryson, who'd always had good taste, had chosen it as a place to live.

Good taste…except in how he'd begun to treat her in their ultimately doomed relationship.

She certainly didn't consider it good taste for him to criticize her work and tell her what to do.

But that was irrelevant now.

"Okay," she finally said, pulling gently on Lorrie's leash so her harness let the pup know where Harper wanted her to go. "We can head inside now."

"Sounds good." Bryson, who was beside her, turned to

go back to the car. He opened the back door of the SUV and pulled out Harper's compact suitcase and one of the large backpacks she had also used to carry some of her things, as well as the small doggy bed she had brought for Lorrie. She smiled at him as she moved around to pick up the other large backpack, plus the smaller one in which she had put Lorrie's supplies, such as her food and water bowls, and some kibble and canned food.

"That everything?" Bryson asked.

Harper interpreted that to mean he was surprised that she could survive on so little. But one backpack she carried contained her laptop computer, and as long as she had that—and had access to Wi-Fi on it and her phone so she could communicate with the world, including all her research resources and her editors—she was just fine.

"It's all I need for now," she told him. Lorrie and she walked with him to the front door of the building, and he used a key card to open it. The lobby was small but nice and included a table with a few chairs, where Harper figured the residents could hang out with visitors. They headed for the two elevators across the room, and Bryson pushed the up button. One of the doors opened right away, and they, plus Lorrie, went inside.

His place was apparently on the second floor, and it didn't take long for the elevator door to open again. "It's at the end of the hall," he told her.

After passing several doors, he used his key card again at the last one, and gestured for Harper to enter. She did, maneuvering with Lorrie and the things she carried.

"Nice place," she said right away, and it was. Of course, she'd figured it was roomy since he had invited her to stay. The living area was wide, with a comfortable-looking beige sofa with a large ottoman facing the television attached to the wall, a matching chair and a clean, shining wooden floor. Shelves along the side wall were filled with books, and Harper figured she would satisfy her curiosity later about what Bryson read. Although a couple with large print along the binding indicated they were about law-enforcement issues such as tactics and criminal enterprises—no surprise.

The only surprise was why he was no longer a cop, although she guessed it might have something to do with his aunt at the doggy day care facility.

"Come on in," he told her although she was already inside. But he led her past the kitchen and down a hallway with a few doors leading off it. She guessed the one at the end must be his bedroom, since he ushered her into one across from the bathroom.

It wasn't very large but contained a queen-sized bed with a fluffy brown coverlet and a couple of large pillows, plus a dresser that had a mirror over it and a small closet. Nice and inviting. A place she wouldn't mind staying for a while, and she was happy when Bryson put Lorrie's doggy bed down on the area rug beside the bed.

She laid her things on top of the bed, and Bryson did the same with the rest. "How about if you unpack later?" he said. "I want us to go back to Barky, but would like to talk for a few minutes first."

He didn't make that a question. And Harper figured she did owe him some answers—like about what her conversation with Macie had been about.

Maybe she could get some answers from him too, regarding why he was here.

"Don't want to take the time to make coffee or tea," he said as they returned to the living room. "Would you like some ice water?"

"Sounds good. And I'll get some water for Lorrie from the sink." She hustled back into the bedroom and removed her dog's water bowl from one of the bags, and in a minute Lorrie, now unleashed, was lapping water from the bowl sitting on the beige tile kitchen floor.

Harper followed Bryson into the living room, holding the glass of water he'd given her and wishing it was something stronger. She didn't feel comfortable about the conversation they were likely to have.

But he had offered to let her live here. To help watch over her until hopefully, sometime soon, she'd be able to move to the safety of the Chance Animal Shelter facility.

Bryson sat on one of the chairs, and Harper planted herself at one end of the sofa. It was fluffy and comfortable, at least.

But she didn't feel relaxed when Bryson started the conversation. "So tell me about that phone call."

She couldn't help staring right at his handsome face. His dark brown eyes were planted directly on her, waiting for her to begin.

And so she did. She explained that Macie was one of the editors she sold a lot of stories to. She also gave more details than before about the threats directed to her there and at other publications.

"So that's why you started looking for someplace else to stay besides your home, where you might be found more easily." His deep voice sounded caring, as it once had when they were a couple, and it made Harper feel warm inside.

But their topic of discussion was anything but warm. "That's right." She mentioned again the security guard at one of the places she'd been researching who described to her the rumored reason for the Chance shelter, how she'd contacted Scott and set up the interview today. "But I understand why he might be uncomfortable with me, since I am in the media. He has no reason to trust that I'll keep everything quiet. But...well, my conversation with Macie today underscored why I need to be at the shelter, if it's what I think it is, if at all possible."

She went on to reveal what Macie had told her about the threats, and about what she'd said about the criticisms about one of Harper's recent articles.

And she couldn't help staring down at her hands, then at Lorrie, as she heard her voice break.

When she'd finished, Bryson asked, "Do you have any idea who might be doing this? Or at least a motive someone might have to physically harm you?"

She shook her head, tears filling her eyes. "Not really, although whoever it is must really hate my stories."

"Well, you'll be safe here," he stated. "I'll make sure of it. And while you're here, we'll look into things, maybe get you situated at the Chance Animal Shelter, but in any case figure out what's going on. And get it all resolved so you won't have to worry about it anymore."

Damn, but that sounded good. Exactly what Harper hoped for. What she needed. But was it possible?

And as much as she'd like to rely on Bryson to help her see it through, get everything in her life back to its usual good self, she simply couldn't count on it.

If only she felt she could fully trust him.

But they'd been close before, until he had become

highly critical about a feature article she had written about a small-town police department in Nevada where the cops had taken over the local animal shelter because it wasn't bringing in all the strays in town. The shelter managers said it was because they hadn't had the room and would have had to kill the strays, but they did work to try to find other locations for them. But the police chief tried to change it, bring the animals in…and do away with those strays.

Harper had written a feature that was critical of the cops, and Bryson, though understanding, and caring about the strays, had thought her article too nasty against the local police. She didn't like him telling her what to do in her field. She didn't tell him how to be a cop, after all, even though there were things he and his department had done that she didn't like and had even considered writing an article about, but hadn't. They'd argued. A lot.

And then she'd stomped away from him.

Now? She still didn't like that argument. But she'd trusted him as a good cop.

Well, she was about to trust him with her life.

"You're awfully quiet," he told her. "Is there anything else you'd like to tell me?"

She didn't want to admit she was thinking about their prior relationship…and breakup. He was being kind now, and the fact they'd once had something between them wasn't relevant.

Although that might be why he'd offered to help her until, hopefully, she got accepted at the Chance Animal Shelter.

"Not really," she replied. "I'm just thinking about why I'm here and hoping it won't be for long." She was surprised to see what appeared to be disappointment on Bryson's face. Was he wanting more than a brief stay here from her?

She certainly didn't want to put him in danger, former cop or not.

As they sat there, Lorrie started walking restlessly around the living room and Bryson put out his hand. Harper's beloved little French bulldog, whom Harper had adopted after Bryson and she broke up, went over and began sniffing his hand, then licking it.

Bryson laughed. "Sweet pup."

"She definitely is." Harper paused. "Would you like to know why her name is Lorrie?"

Bryson looked at her, still smiling, and that expression somehow made Harper all warm and fuzzy inside again. Damn, but she would have to be careful not to allow her emotions go wild, as they had before, around Bryson.

"Sure," he told her.

Good. That was a nice, cute but neutral topic. "Well, as you know she's a French bulldog. She has those big ears, so I decided to name her sort of after them in French. The French word for ear is *oreille*." She pronounced it as closely as she could to the actual pronunciation. "I figured the closest name to that was Lorrie."

"I get it," Bryson said, touching the dog's ears gently. "Hi, Lorrie-ears."

Harper laughed. It certainly felt good to be with Bryson.

It even felt safer than she had considered herself for a while.

If only things went well here, and they both remained safe.

* * *

For the moment, even though he wanted them to head back to Barky, Bryson remained on the chair in his living room near Harper, considering what they'd just talked about.

Well, he'd learned what he needed about her phone call that had gotten her so emotional—and it had been what he'd assumed, even though he previously hadn't known who had called or what had actually been discussed.

But Harper had clearly known the caller, that editor. And they had talked about threats to her—more threats than before.

He would take care of her.

He still hoped Scott would allow her to stay at the shelter for a while, or sort of hoped. He wouldn't see her as much there.

But she would be safer.

In the meantime, he would make a call before they left for Barky so Harper's protection would be increased while she stayed in town too.

Before he could excuse himself to make the call though, Harper said, "I've answered a bunch of your questions, so I'd like for you to answer some of mine now."

Uh-oh. Bryson froze. What would she ask?

Would he want to answer?

Would he answer? Well, he'd have to see.

"What's that?" he asked her, attempting to sound pleased with the idea.

"Why aren't you a cop now?" Her expression, as she studied his face, looked concerned. Did she think he had been hurt? Fired?

Or that he had turned into an unprofessional idiot just leaping from job to job, or not having a job at all? After all, she might recognize he was associated with Barky Boulevard, but didn't know why, except that she had met his aunt there. Maybe she recognized that he was part owner now...or not.

He tried to determine quickly the best way to address her question, and decided to answer truthfully.

"Family matters," he said with a shrug and a slight smile. "Aunt Andrea got into a bit of financial overload, so I decided to help out. And, well, since it wasn't clear what had caused the problems, I decided to come here to work at least for a while, and not just send her money."

This wasn't a good time to get into how the rest of the family, like his mom and uncle, practically begged him to come and take care of Andrea. One of them might have been able to move here, but he had a reputation for not only caring a lot for animals, and his family, but also knowing how to take charge.

Plus, Andrea and he had always gotten along well, even when he was a little kid, and later when he'd joined the army.

And money? Well, he didn't have a lot as a veteran and cop, but he knew how to handle it.

"That's really sweet of you," Harper said, admiration in her expression. And more?

Heck, no. What had been between them was long over. She'd never forgive him for criticizing how she handled at least one of her well-publicized stories that condemned a police force for how it treated an animal shelter and how it handled homeless dogs that were brought in...or not brought in.

"Anyway," he continued, "things seem to be improving at Barky, and my aunt seems happy. I think I'm helping to figure out how we can make it more successful, and when it is I intend to return to LA and my cop job, assuming it's still available. If not, I'll attempt to find something else in law enforcement."

"Got it," Harper said.

And since he let her know he hadn't fully abandoned his cop background, maybe she'd feel a little safer in his presence.

All he had to do was keep her safe.

Right now, he needed to make that phone call outside her presence. He said, "Let's head for Barky soon, but right now I want to take a quick walk outside the condo, just to make sure everything looks okay."

"Do you think whoever is after me knows I'm here?" Harper sounded shocked.

"Nope, I've no reason to think that. Just being careful." *And making that phone call I don't intend to tell you about*, he thought, but she'd figure it out later anyway if everything went well.

"Okay," she said. But she didn't really sound okay.

In a minute, he'd left the condo and gone into the hallway, after giving Lorrie, who'd followed him to the door, a pat. While he was out there, he did walk down the hall to the end and looked out the window there.

Everything looked fine, as he anticipated. The condo development was a nice one, and he didn't believe anything unsafe was going on.

Although—well, not knowing the source of the threats against Harper did concern him, so he would be careful anywhere.

And it was time to make that phone call, to Chance Police Chief Andrew Shermovski. No one else was in the hallway, but, leaning against the wall beside the window, Bryson kept his tone low, so no one could eavesdrop from inside one of the units.

He got through right away. "Hi, Bryson," Sherm said. "Everything okay at Barky Boulevard?"

"Yes, I'm glad to say—and I want to keep it that way. Any chance you, or maybe Assistant Chief Province if you're not available, can come to Barky this afternoon? I want to introduce you to someone who's in some trouble. She might get to stay at the shelter, but Scott is still deciding about that, and I want to make sure she remains safe while in town."

"What's the story?" Sherm sounded wholly professional, and Bryson figured it would be a good thing for him to know Harper's situation, so he told him.

"Although the people at Barky aren't being told who she is, she's a well-known journalist who's been receiving threats. She came here after hearing rumors about Chance Animal Shelter, but because she has a public following Scott's taking his time about accepting her. Meanwhile, I've put my cop hat back on and am watching over her, but I'm not sure I'm enough. I want the local PD to meet her and maybe help me keep her safe."

"Got it. Well, I'm not able to come this afternoon, but I will send Kara if she's available. And then we'll see if we can help."

"Perfect. Thanks a lot."

They soon hung up, and Bryson returned to the condo. Time to head to Barky Boulevard.

Chapter 5

As they left the condo headed for her car, with Lorrie leashed beside her as usual, Harper couldn't help wondering what Bryson had been up to when he'd left his unit—*their* unit, for the moment—then returned. He'd indicated he was simply being cautious in his looking after her, and she appreciated it.

But was that really what he'd been up to? If so, why not elaborate more when he'd said he was leaving for a short while?

Could she trust him to be honest with her?

Maybe she shouldn't after the way their relationship had ended, but, damn it, she did.

After all, she might not have agreed with him, or the way he wound up criticizing her, but she could understand why a cop would take the other cops' side in a dispute.

Even if it had hurt her feelings. A lot. And made her angry on behalf of the unknown animals involved.

She could only hope she wasn't wrong now in trusting Bryson. In any case, she would do all she could to take care of herself.

And Lorrie, of course.

Harper noticed Bryson acting coplike and staying

close to her while scouting their area outside the condo development with his gaze, even though she didn't see anyone else around. She supposed that was because it was midafternoon, and most people would be at their jobs, or working from home.

And if they did happen to see anyone, it could just be a neighbor. Whoever was threatening her surely couldn't know her current location since she hadn't told anyone where she was heading.

Well, anyone but Scott, and she certainly didn't suspect he was the one who'd been threatening her. Quite the contrary.

And even though she trusted Bryson to help take care of her, the idea of hiding in a special shelter for a while as she attempted to figure out—remotely—what was going on seemed best.

Maybe.

For now she would have to accept what was going on and do what she could to communicate more with Scott.

Unless, of course, she figured out who was after her, or claiming to be, and found a way to stop it. Stop him...or her. Maybe even find a way to have that person arrested.

And best yet, also make sure to write some articles that let the world know what a horrible menace that person was. Get retribution of sorts for what she was going through.

She smiled grimly as they reached her car in the partially filled outdoor parking lot, with her mind wrapped up in who she was and how she could best help herself eventually, she hoped.

"You okay?" Bryson's sharp words beside her brought her back to reality.

"Of course," she told him, as he opened the back door of her car and ushered Lorrie inside. Harper took over strapping her pup in for safety, and when she backed away she saw that Bryson was right behind her, scouting their environment even more. "Who's driving?" she asked. He still had her key fob from when he'd ridden with her here earlier and used her key to help get things out of the car.

"Me. I know the way back to Barky Boulevard the best."

"Yes," she said. "You do." But he could always direct her there. When they had been together before, he hadn't acted all man-in-charge. Depending on where they were going on their dates, and when, she'd sometimes driven them.

And in some ways she wondered if it wouldn't be safer for her now if she drove and he continued to watch the world around them, and be prepared to react if he saw something wrong.

She had no doubts he would continue to be observant and do what needed to be done if he happened to see some kind of danger.

In any case, it didn't really hurt to let this off-duty cop take charge. Take care of her. Make sure she stayed safe.

Make sure they both stayed safe, since she'd never get over it, would hate herself, if whoever was threatening her wound up harming Bryson because he was protecting her.

She tried to watch carefully as he drove them from the parking lot and onto the street beyond the condo development, then toward downtown Chance. She needed to learn her way around, even if she wasn't going to be in this area long, or at least she hoped not. No matter how long she remained in Chance, but not in the shelter, it would be better if she was in the highly secure area where the shelter was located, not far from downtown.

She generally knew its location since she had done her homework before coming here and had checked out online the highly reputed Chance Animal Shelter, but she hadn't gone there first. Instead, she had headed for Barky Boulevard, for her meeting with Scott, figuring she would wind up at the shelter later today after he accepted her. Right.

But it was around a park area, from what she could tell. And the picture shown online had indicated it was secured behind a very tall wooden fence, which made sense for an animal shelter, and even more for the kind of shelter it probably was.

Now… "Could you drive us past the Chance Animal Shelter before we go to Barky Boulevard?" She had to at least ask. "I'd really like to see it."

"Guess that would be okay," Bryson said, making her smile broadly. He glanced over at her and smiled back… until his expression turned into a frown. "That's assuming you're not intending to write anything about it, even its animal rescue part. Not unless Scott agrees. Right?"

"Of course," she said. And she meant it. She loved doing feature articles about all kinds of animal-related places, but she knew better than to provide any kind of publicity to this particular one right now, and maybe never.

"Okay, then," Bryson said, slowing a bit as if preparing to make a turn off the downtown street they were on, with lots of retail stores on it. "But on one condition."

Uh-oh. "What's that?" she asked hesitantly.

"Let's talk about what you do and who you think could be making those threats."

She snorted a brief laugh. "The first part is easy, and you already know most of it. I write feature articles involving animals, including rescues and even wildlife when I come up with ideas I can research, and I sell them primarily to three magazines. One is *Puppies, Kittens and Humans*, where Macie is the editor, and the others are *Pup Rescue Forever* and *Pets and Love*." She sort of hated mentioning *Pup Rescue Forever* since it had been the subject of the controversy Macie had mentioned, but it was one of Harper's main publications, or at least had been before. She would need to contact the editor, Wanda Grey, soon to make sure things were still okay between them. The editor of *Pets and Love*, Betsy Bordley too. Whenever she felt able to contact people out there in the world again. "I also sell articles sometimes to larger national publications about dogs or cats," she continued, "and even magazines published by some of the large rescue organizations that have sites at various places throughout the country. Newspapers occasionally too." She named a few, and he nodded.

"That's pretty much what I thought. You and I might have lost touch, but I remained interested in what you did so I tried to read some of the articles you've written. You're easy to find online."

She gave a real laugh this time. "I'm delighted to hear that." Not that she wasn't aware of it. And proud of it.

In fact, she was very proud of the career she had chosen for herself, and the success she'd had writing and selling so many articles—enough that she easily supported herself.

Before, at least. She still had to continue writing, staying remote without divulging where she was writing from.

At least she was able to create and sell her features remotely. Even research them, to some extent, although doing a lot in person was preferable—often more interesting to her and to her readers, and she could take better photographs of what she was writing about rather than finding examples online and getting permission to use them.

"Okay, then," Bryson said after he made a turn. The street they were on now was similar to the last one, although the stores lining it were smaller, with more space between. Likely getting farther from the center of town. "Next question, though we've talked about it before. Who do you think is threatening you?"

Harper couldn't help laughing again, this time aware she didn't sound at all happy. "I wish I knew. I've been pondering various possibilities. Maybe it was someone involved with the article Macie mentioned, where I've been criticized for getting things wrong about the Pet Me For Life Shelter, although I don't believe I did. And if I was in my normal life, I'd dive in and look into it. But, well, not sure how I can do it now, from a distance. And I haven't been able to figure out why the people involved with that shelter would threaten my life anyway, even if I did make some mistakes in my article. I'd like to revisit the article, but I don't believe I said anything too derogatory about the place. I sometimes criticize the shelters I research, but I only come down hard on those that 'euthanize' animals they can't find new homes for, and that's a misnomer, since euthanizing mostly means humanely killing an animal that's suffering. Sure, they may be suffering for not being part of a family, but it's not humane to kill them just because they're homeless."

"I agree with that," Bryson said, glancing at her with a nod, then back toward the road. Interesting, since his attitude toward the cops dealing with strays way back when might have been different. "Who else might be after you?"

She wished she knew. It wasn't as if she hadn't been thinking hard about possibilities, but none really made sense. She'd considered some of her primary rivals, other writers who got a lot of articles published about dogs and cats and rescues and her other chief focuses, like wildlife. She'd come up with a few who might like to get her out of the business so they could get more stories published. But threaten her?

Nevertheless, to keep their conversation going, she told Bryson, "I guess some of the writers I consider my closest competition might have something against me, since I do tend to sell more stories than any of them. But I doubt they'd be the ones to threaten me that way."

"Unless they could find a way to hurt you and write their own stories about it, right?"

She took a deep breath. "I guess anything is possible, but—"

"Tell me some names. I'll ask you to do it again later and will write them down, make sure they're investigated, just in case."

Investigated? By whom, she wondered. He didn't say

he'd be the one to do that investigating, although maybe that was what he'd meant.

"I've thought of a few, but the ones I consider my greatest competition go by the names Edna Dogmom, Dierdre Trotsen and Roger Eddella. You might have heard of any or all of them, since you said you're reading my articles and maybe you're reading others that have some similarities."

"They all do sound somewhat familiar. I'll check them out, and any others whose names you give me."

Then he would be doing the checking, or at least some of it. But who else did he have in mind?

Well, hopefully things would become clearer as whatever he did progressed.

"And who else have you thought of who might be threatening you?" he asked.

"Not many others. Although I do criticize some shelters and rescuers if they're actually doing things that allow animals to suffer, like 'euthanizing' them, killing them just because they're difficult to rehome." She sort of sang the word *euthanizing* and knew Bryson would understand why she still despised that word, considering how it had been at the center of their prior cop-related dispute that had ended their relationship. "I haven't written recently about any places that are especially brutal, preferring to let my readers celebrate the good things about rescue animals and those who do the rescuing."

"Got it. Anyway, look out the window. I'm not slowing down much since we need to get to Barky, but there's the Chance Animal Shelter. From what I understand, it used to be a large apartment complex that was enclosed and redone to become the shelter." He took one hand off the steering wheel and waved toward the area to their right, which seemed to be a couple of city blocks enclosed by a tall wooden fence that had no openings. They did pass by a closed gate with a sign on it that identified the place as the Chance Animal Shelter, and it appeared to have a box outside that people could open, presumably with electronics inside it that would allow visitors to communicate with those in the shelter to let them in, Harper assumed. And as they continued circling, Harper saw a parking area outside with several parked cars.

"Looks like a nice, safe place for the animals they're rescuing," Harper said, "and maybe even some people." She kept her tone light so he would know she was kidding. It didn't look outside like a people shelter, but presumably inside people in trouble could be sheltered well, along with animals, if things inside the fence were as protective as the appearance of the outside.

"Yeah, that's what I've heard." Bryson turned the car to veer back downtown. "And maybe someday you'll find out."

That might be the best thing for her, Bryson figured—assuming her claims of threats were real, and not just a way for her to get inside the shelter to research it. And he'd had a short amount of time to get to know her again and didn't believe that was the case.

Although he would continue to observe her when he could to make sure that was true.

"So we're on our way to Barky Boulevard?" Harper asked, her head turned toward the window where the shelter was now disappearing from view.

"Yep." He wanted to hurry there since it wasn't too

long until the appointment he had set up for later that afternoon. Fortunately, though, he knew Aunt Andrea was okay with running things, just not finances.

They were now cruising along one of the main streets downtown, and Bryson soon made a turn into the alley behind Barky, parking in one of the designated spots. "Here we are."

They entered, and Bryson immediately went to where Aunt Andrea was sitting on a chair observing the dogs of different sizes on the floor now being played with by a couple of the employees—everything from Scout, the border collie mix, to Mama, a Chihuahua mix, to Bugs, a part German shepherd. Bryson had played with them all before too. They all looked familiar. Sounded familiar too, as they barked when Cindy and Ellie, the employees, threw toy balls and told them to fetch.

"Hi, Andrea," Bryson said.

"Hi, Bryson," she said in return.

Bryson turned to Harper. "Hanna, would you like to get down on the floor and play with the pups?" That was partly to remind her, and his aunt in case she knew who Harper really was, what her identity here should be.

"Sure," she said. She put the small purse she was carrying onto a chair and got down on her knees.

Bryson checked his phone to see the time. They had another ten minutes, fortunately. He also started playing ball with some of the dogs. But in five minutes he got off his knees and headed to the front door.

As expected, Assistant Police Chief Kara Province was there. In her black uniform, of course. She was a pretty lady, with short, black hair and dark brown eyes that now surveyed Bryson's face.

"Hi, Kara," he said immediately. "Thanks for coming."

"Sherm said you had a situation here and wanted the Chance PD to meet someone," she responded.

"Exactly," Bryson said. "Please, come in."

He moved aside, and she entered the Barky premises and did like everyone else when they came in. She stood a moment, looking around the room at dogs playing all over the floor, employees encouraging and taking care of them.

"This place is so cute," she said. "Makes me wish as I always do that I had a dog. But with my job I wouldn't have adequate time to take care of one."

"Well, you could always adopt a new family member to hang out with you at home, but bring the pup here during the days while you're at work."

"That sounds wonderful, if I only worked days. But I'm on the job a lot during evenings and weekends too. But you've gotten my mind rolling again. Maybe someday…"

"Meanwhile, you're always welcome to come here and visit and play when you get a chance. And right now—"

"Right now, let's meet with whoever it is you think needs the attention of the police. Someone who's not at the Chance Animal Shelter, I gather."

"Scott's still considering her, thanks to her difficult circumstances, but— Well, you'll see. With her background, he's a bit concerned she might be too outspoken about what the shelter's really about, although I think she can be trusted. Anyway, yeah. Come on into my office, then I'll go get her."

Kara edged her way along with him, clearly attempting not to garner much human attention despite her uniform. Bryson figured the employees still might recognize that "Hanna" had a reason to meet with the cop since she'd soon need to join them. They'd have to come up with some acceptable reason, like she wanted to discuss a missing relative who'd lived in Chance.

Right. That made sense. He'd have to tell her about it soon.

After Kara was situated, Bryson maneuvered his way back through the crowd of busy dogs and their human playmates until he was close to his target, who used a braided toy to play tug-of-war with Jello, a golden retriever mix. Her own dog joined in, jumping at the rope.

He didn't have to do much to get the attention of "Hanna."

"I've got something to talk to you about," he soon said, in case anyone was listening.

She'd clearly seen who'd gone into his office, or at least Kara's uniform. "Then let's go talk," she said, standing and handing the toy to one of the other employees, who took it and began playing with Jello.

And Harper, with Lorrie, preceded him to his office.

Chapter 6

Harper had noticed before the entry of the police officer now waiting in Bryson's office. A female cop, and judging by the insignia on her jacket she might not just be a regular officer. Harper had, after all, interviewed top law-enforcement brass in other areas, and she recognized some of the symbolism. Two stars were on this woman's uniform, and that might mean she was a deputy police chief. For the town of Chance?

Well, hopefully Harper—no, *Hanna*—would find out soon. And also learn why she was here.

Had there been threats made around town because of Harper's presence somehow?

"Harper, this is Assistant Police Chief Kara Province. Kara, this is Harper, the woman I wanted you to meet. Around here, we're calling her Hanna. She's kind of undercover, since she has been receiving some threats."

Harper watched Kara come toward her with her hand out, so she also approached and shook it. Lorrie was right beside her, and the assistant chief then bent down and held her hand out to the pup, who, instead of shaking it, licked it. Kara laughed. "Good to meet both of you," she said.

Was it really? Harper wondered. Again, she wanted to know what the assistant chief was doing here.

She found out soon, after Bryson encouraged them to take seats facing his desk, which he sat behind.

"If you're receiving threats," Kara said right away, sitting beside Harper and facing her, "I assume you're here to move to the Chance Animal Shelter." She glanced toward Bryson. "She's aware of what it is, right?"

"Yes, and Scott is still considering whether she can become a staff member there. But so you know, Kara, Harper is a journalist, in the public eye, so Scott is concerned about whether she'll get word out there about what the shelter really is—"

"But I've assured him," Harper interrupted, "that I have no intention of doing that." She looked at Kara. "I write a lot about animal and rescue facilities and more, in a lot of publications, and if I wrote anything at all about the shelter that would be my focus. And I'd run anything by Scott. I've no intention of making the underlying purpose of the facility public. And why would I, especially if I'm one of the people living there under their protection?"

"That sounds sensible," Kara said.

"For now," Bryson said, "until Scott feels comfortable letting Harper live at the shelter, she's staying with me, here in town."

"Then you, with your cop background, are protecting her," Kara asserted, nodding. "Makes sense."

"Yeah, I am. And hopefully whoever has been threatening Harper has no idea where she is. But she's just had contact with at least one of the editors she works with, who told her their publication has received recent threatening emails about Harper, so apparently whoever was menacing her before is still trying. She doesn't know who or where that person is. And as you know, I'm here to help run Barky Boulevard, not as a cop. That's why I contacted Sherm, and why he sent you here to meet Harper."

So that was some explanation, Harper thought. But did it indicate Bryson would have some help in watching over her?

Apparently it did.

"Got it," Kara said. "And the Chance PD can help, at least a bit. We always have patrols driving around town, but I'll get Sherm's okay, and we can have even more go by here at Barky Boulevard and wherever you live, Bryson."

"That's what I was hoping," he said.

"You'll need to let us know, though," Kara said, "if Harper hears anything else, gets any more information."

"Definitely," Harper said, breathing a sigh of relief. She knew Bryson well enough to feel comfortable he would do all in his power to protect her. As a cop, he knew a lot. But since he wasn't an official cop here, his resources would be limited, even if his bravery wasn't.

It would certainly help to know that the local police force had his back. And hers.

"Great," Bryson said. "That was why I wanted Sherm, or you, to meet Harper, see that she's basically an okay person with a problem, even if Scott doesn't trust her yet. But having the Chance PD as a potential resource just in case Harper's problems follow her here could be a great help."

"Oh, yes," Harper said, looking straight into Kara's

serious brown eyes. "Thank you so much! I really appreciate those extra patrols." To watch over Bryson as well as her. "And I definitely hope it's unnecessary."

"Well, so will we," Kara said. "And having patrols visible in the area might help keep it that way."

"That's as it should be," Bryson agreed. "Oh, and if you could provide a temporary license plate for Harper's car that whoever is after her couldn't identify, that would be great."

"Good idea," Kara said. She rose then, and so did Lorrie, who'd been lying at Harper's feet. Kara laughed and kneeled to pet the dog. When she stood up again she said, "Time to head back to the station and arrange for those patrols." She looked at Bryson. "Write down your address for me so we can increase the night patrols around there."

Bryson opened his middle desk drawer and drew out a notecard and pen. He jotted something down and handed the card to Kara. "Here it is."

She looked at it. "Nice condo development," she said.

"I like it," Bryson agreed.

So did Harper so far, but she didn't say anything.

"I think I'll come back here now and then too, to play with your dog and maybe some of the others. And I might just pop up to the Chance Animal Shelter to talk to Scott…and check out some of the dogs there for adoption."

"That sounds wonderful," Harper said, meaning both of the ideas Kara had mentioned.

"And I'd like for you to point me to some of the articles on dogs you've written," she told Harper. "Sounds fun."

"Definitely. Do you have an email address where I can send you links?"

"Sure." Kara took the card Bryson had given her and tore it in half. She wrote something down, and when she handed it to Harper, it did indeed contain an email address, ending in *chancepd*.

"I'll send you something soon," Harper promised. "And thank you so much."

Kara headed out of the office, and Bryson followed. So did Harper, with Lorrie. It again amused her to see Kara play with some of the dogs, many of whom were leaping around, barking while playing with some of the employees. Noisy, but fun.

Harper even had an urge to join in—which she would, later. Now, she just watched.

So did Bryson, who stood closer to the middle of the excitement.

The assistant chief seemed to really like the pups here, and she'd said she might be open to adopting a dog someday.

She apparently was a caring person. And good at what she did in law enforcement, since she helped to run the local police department.

Harper wasn't surprised that her mind immediately began constructing a possible article about Assistant Chief Kara Province, but it would remain in her mind for now. She couldn't do anything to notify the world about where she was at the moment. Maybe later, when things here settled down and she felt comfortable about being "Hanna" and helping at Barky Boulevard…and being protected by Bryson and, to some extent, the Chance PD. It might not hurt sometime in the future to make it public that she had been here, as long as it appeared she wasn't any longer.

And that would likely work out even better if she became a temporary resident of the Chance Animal Shelter.

No articles about the reality of that place, though, as she'd already made clear—despite her journalistic mind again focusing on some interesting angles that she could never make public.

If only she could get back to her regular life. And she would…someday. When she was safe.

She watched as Kara finally said goodbye and headed for the day care center's outside door, with Bryson following and speaking with her.

Standing just outside the office with Lorrie, Harper wondered what they were saying. She figured her ears should be ringing, since they were probably discussing her and her situation.

Later today, after she'd done her duties as an apparent employee of Barky Boulevard, and once they got home to Bryson's, she would get on her computer. Contact the editors she worked with most, including Macie again.

Find out if any of them had heard about any more threats to her.

And she would, of course, check her own email for anything upsetting.

If all seemed well, could she start getting ready to return to her real world?

Too soon after just arriving here, she figured. And her conversation with Macie had made it appear even more unlikely.

And as weird as it seemed, she didn't exactly want to go back to how things used to be, before the threats.

Not now, when she was once again in close contact with Bryson.

Foolish? Maybe. But maybe fate had intervened in this miserable way to bring them back together.

But he seemed determined to also help her get accepted by Scott as a resident of the Chance Animal Shelter, and that did make sense—even though Harper would undoubtedly see even less of him again, if at all.

She sighed and pursed her lips, hoping that no one but Lorrie was watching her.

She didn't want any people to recognize how worried and nervous she was about her current situation… and the future.

Okay, time to tackle the reason for her being here. "Come, Lorrie," she said, and they carefully walked through the crowd of other dogs, with Lorrie sniffing and trying to play, until they reached where Andrea was playing with a few.

"Can we join you?"

"Sure, Hanna. And Lorrie." Bryson's aunt soon got them included in the nearby games.

"Thanks for coming, Kara," Bryson said to the assistant police chief as he followed her to the parking lot. "And thanks in advance for any help you can provide around here, like those extra patrols we were talking about."

"You're welcome in advance." The attractive cop smiled at Bryson, then looked a little concerned. "Any idea what you're going to tell your aunt and employees about why the Assistant Police Chief happened to visit, and talk to you?"

"Already figured that out. I'll just tell them that the city's Animal Services Department has a few dogs who need some special care, and you came to talk about that. As to why Hanna joined us…well, I was thinking one reason we could say she was here was that she was trying to find a missing relative who might be in Chance, so she wanted to talk to the police."

"Right. I can always say the department is trying to help her find that relative. And this doggy day care place can help take care of those dogs until they're taken in by Chance Animal Services or found homes. Anyway, I'll stay in touch with you and with Scott about what he decides about Harper/Hanna. And I'm sure Sherm will keep in contact about it all too. Meanwhile, I'm interested in learning more about Harper. I gather she will send me information about the articles she publishes, but I figure researching her online will come up with at least some of them."

"I'm sure it will."

They said their goodbyes, and Kara drove off in the police car she had parked in the Barky Boulevard parking lot.

When Bryson returned inside, he watched what was going on while standing just inside the door, as he often did. It was always enjoyable, watching his aunt and their employees giving the dogs commands, tossing rubber animals for them to follow and bring back, playing tug-of-war with braided toys and whatever else was happening.

Somehow, he enjoyed even more watching Harper act as one of those employees, playing with their canine charges of the day, as well as her own cute, energetic dog.

He approached Harper. She glanced up at him, and he gestured unobtrusively for her to follow. She got the message and stood up, still playing a little.

He went into his office, and she soon joined him with Lorrie. She shut the door behind them.

"Is everything okay with Kara, and the Chance PD keeping an eye on things around me?"

She sounded concerned, and he recognized that she must have seen him follow Kara outside for a few minutes.

"Yes, all's well, and Kara is looking forward to reading some of your published articles."

Harper laughed, the sound almost musical in Bryson's mind. Not surprising, coming from such an attractive woman who'd once meant so much to him. "I'll send her some links soon."

"Great," he said. "And now that you're here, I want for us to call Scott."

He waved toward the chairs facing his desk, and Harper sat in one of them, concerned.

"Have you heard anything from him? Is he still considering me as a potential resident of the Chance Shelter?"

"I'd imagine so, but we can ask him. I just want to let him know our latest communications with the Chance PD though. He's still one of their cops and I'm sure he'll want to know that you're going to be partly under their protection as well."

Harper relaxed in her chair, and Bryson pulled his phone out of his hip pocket and pressed in Scott's number, then put it on speaker.

"Hi, Bryson," Scott answered right away. "Everything okay?"

He didn't mention Harper, but Bryson felt certain the woman he was with was also on Scott's mind.

"Sure is. In fact, Assistant Police Chief Kara just visited us here at Barky Boulevard to meet Harper and Lorrie. Since I'm the kind-of undercover cop here watching over them, I'd asked Sherm if the Chance PD could send some extra patrols around while Harper was here, to make sure all seemed okay, and Kara appeared fine with the idea. I know they already send patrols around the Chance Animal Shelter too. But in case their additional protection here made it easier for you to decide whether Harper could become a staff member there, I figured we'd let you know."

"We? Then is Harper there with you?"

Bryson held the phone in her direction, and she said, "Yes I am, Scott. And, well, even though things here seem fine, and even better with extra police protection—"

"Yeah, you want to know if you can move in here," he said. "I understand that. In fact…well, Bryson, could you maybe bring Harper for a visit tomorrow? I can show her around, and we can talk some more, and I'll hopefully be able to give her an answer sooner."

"Fine with me," Bryson said,

"And with me," Harper agreed, and Bryson grinned at her.

"Make it late morning, if that's possible," Scott said.

And that became part of Bryson's schedule for tomorrow…as well as the woman he was protecting.

Chapter 7

Tomorrow. Harper thought about what would happen then as she left Bryson in his office. She hurried, Lorrie at her side, through the dogs along the floor, careful not to step on any, and across the room to get closer to Andrea... and play with some of those dogs, as "Hanna" should do. And wanted to do while she was here.

Harper, as herself, wanted to talk to Bryson more about how things would go tomorrow, but she could do that later.

Right now, she wanted to think, while having fun playing with the energetic pups at the same time, to help relieve her stress.

Still... Harper would get to visit the Chance Animal Shelter tomorrow. Have an opportunity to convince Scott she was legitimate, needed protection from whoever was threatening her, in case they happened to figure out where she currently was.

First though, she wanted to check her emails. Make sure there were no additional threats, even though that might make her being here feel less necessary. But until she, and her editors on her behalf, didn't receive any for a long time, hopefully never again, she just couldn't feel safe, so being here felt crucial.

She also wanted to attempt to contact those editors now to see if they'd heard anything else, and especially to contact Wanda Grey, her editor at *Pup Rescue Forever*, the publication where Macie had said the critiques of her most recent article had been horrible. Not that the threats were a result of that, but Harper wanted to do everything possible to ensure she could still submit to that magazine, and have her articles published there.

Maybe, once she was in a position to see those bad reviews, she would be able to figure out a way to address them. Fix whatever had gone wrong. Assuming something had, and it wasn't just a scam created by whoever was threatening her in other ways.

First, she needed to see those reviews and any other correspondence she'd received from her editors, fans and anyone else. Tonight? Maybe. In any event, she wanted to take some time on her computer to see what she could. Maybe contact Wanda and ask her opinion about what had gone on at her magazine.

Perhaps contact some of her other editors too, including Macie, although she wasn't sure what she would say right now. But keeping in touch should be good.

And she couldn't just hang out in Bryson's office at the moment and see what she could accomplish by using her phone rather than her computer. She had a job to do here, as Hanna. And Andrea and the employees probably already considered her an oddball as a Barky Boulevard employee.

Right now, she maneuvered her way around a white

pit bull and a smaller dog, maybe a Maltese mix. And they were also playing with a dachshund.

Lorrie seemed totally happy to join in as Harper got on her knees near where Andrea was playing with a different pit bull and a Cavalier King Charles spaniel.

And Harper had a delightful time taking on the role she was supposed to here, tossing toys and enjoying other doggy games, including with Lorrie.

"Looks like you're enjoying yourself," a deep voice said from over her shoulder. She looked up and unsurprisingly saw Bryson standing there.

"I am. Catch." She threw a squeaky rubber mouse up at him, and he caught it.

He even got down on the floor between his aunt and her, and they both helped to entertain the animals.

Andrea clapped at them and called out, also tossing toys that the dogs chased. But soon, some other people walked into the day care center from the outer door, and Andrea rose and met up with them. They all began taking their dogs home.

The day was finally over, or at least nearly so.

"So are you about ready to leave?" Bryson asked, standing up beside Harper.

She nodded and also drew herself to her feet. Lorrie remained beside her, even though Harper had removed her leash to allow her to have more fun playing. She'd stuffed it into her pocket, and took it out now to attach it again.

She and Bryson said their goodbyes to Andrea and the other employees still there, then went outside. Harper walked slowly at first so Lorrie could take care of what she needed to, and then they walked to the parking lot.

Soon, they were in Harper's car, Bryson driving again. "Pizza okay for dinner?" he asked.

"Sounds good." She'd need to start eating healthy again, but for now whatever was easiest was best. At least they also ordered salads to go at the pizza place, and Harper wondered if Bryson kept any vegetables or salads at his condo to eat when he was alone.

Well, that was his business. And considering his slim, though muscular, physique, she figured he ate healthfully enough. Probably exercised too—did more than just play with dogs.

But he was a cop when he wasn't here, so he undoubtedly kept in shape for that job, like when she had known him before.

Harper watched the streets and sidewalks around them, and realized that Bryson was doing the same thing, obviously making sure they weren't being watched or followed.

Should Harper feel safe? Well, she didn't. Not yet. And maybe not ever.

Although she could always hope that the threats had already stopped.

She needed to check her emails on her phone more often for further threats, or any correspondence from her editors. Had she been avoiding looking out of fear of what she'd see there? Maybe so.

They soon stopped at a restaurant not far from Barky Boulevard in downtown Chance, and they both went inside to pick up the pizza. Lorrie went in with Harper, and fortunately, no one said anything. And Harper maneuvered around and managed to pay for the dinner at the cash register at the end of the restaurant's glass counter.

"Hey," Bryson said, apparently intending to protest.

"Don't give me a hard time," Harper replied, keeping her voice low. "You're watching out for me, and I'm staying at your place and paying no rent. This is the least I can do, and you can be sure I'll do it again."

"But—" Bryson began, but Harper walked around him and took the large pizza box from the server behind the counter.

"You can carry the salad," she told Bryson, and she headed for the busy restaurant's door, Lorrie still at her feet.

At her car, Harper put the pizza in through the ATV's back area so Lorrie couldn't get to it. They got back into the car and arrived at Bryson's condo soon.

They ate pizza and drank some nice red wine that Bryson had, giving Harper another reason to pay for their meal.

And she managed, as they ate, to discuss what they'd do and say the next day when they headed into the Chance Animal Shelter, and she had an opportunity to talk with Scott.

"How well do you know Scott?" Harper asked, holding a slice of pizza in her hand but waiting to take another bite. The one she'd already eaten, with pepperoni and cheese, had tasted good.

She knew that Bryson was acquainted with Scott, and that her off-duty cop protector here also spent some time at the Chance Animal Shelter helping to keep an eye on things there, or at least he and Scott had indicated that.

"Not well, since I only arrived in Chance a few months ago. But as a currently inactive cop I visited the Chance PD first thing and talked with Sherm, the chief, and told him who I was and what I was doing in town. He asked if I'd like to help out now and then at a very special place in the area, and after I promised to keep it secret he told me about the Chance Animal Shelter, then called Scott while I was still in his office. That was the first time I spoke with Scott. He invited me to visit and I learned more about what the shelter actually was, and I've visited more and helped out a few times since then with some staff members in trouble—that's what they call those in protective custody there. So, yeah, I know that's a long explanation of how well I know Scott, but I like him and trust him, and I think he trusts me."

"Makes sense," Harper said. "And does he trust you enough to believe what you say about other people… like me?"

"Hopefully. We'll find out more tomorrow."

So it sounded as if she'd be visiting there with someone who not only knew what the place was about, but also helped out there.

Someone she definitely trusted, at the moment.

Bryson looked at her, putting the slice of pizza he'd been holding back down in his plate. His expression appeared more than serious. Angry? Commanding? "But I don't want you to spoil that trust," he said, "by betraying me and the shelter and writing one of your damn articles about the place."

Damn articles? Didn't he like at least some of what she wrote? She glared at him. "I think we know each other well enough for you to trust me too. I've said I won't write anything about the shelter's underlying purpose, and I won't even write about the animal shelter part without running it by Scott."

"So you've said." He reached down for his pizza slice and took another bite. At least this time his tone had seemed more moderate.

"And I mean it," she stated, realizing she must sound defiant.

But it still earned her a smile from Bryson.

Bryson believed her.

Even though he realized he must have looked skeptical a moment ago, he'd cared for her once, despite how things had gone wrong. And he did appreciate her writing…mostly.

He knew she was relying on him—assuming she really was in trouble. And why would she lie about that?

She'd certainly acted nervous and concerned since she arrived here.

Well, he'd keep an open mind, but assume, for now, that she truly was in trouble.

After all, hadn't he already taken on her protection?

And he'd seen her reaction to that phone call with, apparently, one of her editors who knew some of what was happening.

To keep their conversation going, he said, "So are you working on any articles now?" Like, remotely. If so, how was she researching them? She'd spent a lot of time researching her stories in the past, when they'd been together, mostly in person.

"I'm always writing," she said with a toothy and teasing grin that somehow made her already lovely face even more appealing. "But you know that."

"Yeah, I do," he said. "But in the old days you also

spent a lot of time researching, visiting shelters and zoos and animal people for interviews all the time."

Her expression fell. "Yeah. Things are a bit different at the moment. I'm not surprised you realize that too. But once things settle down a bit here, especially if I wind up at the shelter with no one paying much attention to me, I'll do more remote and virtual research. Maybe here too, if I'm around for a while, though that would work out better if I can hang out in your condo rather than at Barky Boulevard." She paused, then looked back into his face with her green eyes sparkling. "Or, we can think of an excuse for me not to play with the pups there at Barky so much. I could hide in your office with my computer and do some of my real work as Harper, temporarily not being Hanna."

"That might work," Bryson agreed. In fact, she might be safer there by herself, away from the crowd of dogs as well as the people who could come in any time and leave their pups…or otherwise check out the place. And the people there.

Including Harper.

"I like that idea," she said. "But— Well, a lot will depend on how things go during my conversation with Scott tomorrow."

"Right." Bryson wondered if he would be included in it. At least part of it.

He'd want to hear the discussion. Get a sense of Scott's thoughts.

Maybe even put his two cents worth in to support Harper—even though, if all went well, he'd see a lot less of her.

But she hopefully would be safer.

They finished their dinner. He stood to begin taking their dishes to the sink, but once again Harper outmaneuvered him. This time she even rinsed the dishes and loaded them in his dishwasher.

She did, however, allow him to take care of placing the leftover pizza slices in a container and put it into the refrigerator.

And soon they were alone together after dinner. With time before heading to bed.

Separately, but what a shame.

He realized he was again—still—attracted to this smart, beautiful woman.

"So would you like to watch some TV now? Or—"

"I'm sure you won't be surprised to hear that what I want to do is disappear into my bedroom and spend some time on my computer, doing some research."

"And checking your emails for any new threats, right?"

A hint of fear showed up on her face, but she quickly erased it, brave woman that she was.

But he realized that, if all of this was in fact a sham, her expression could be part of that. He'd also learned she could be a good actress if needed for researching her stories.

And, in fact, she was as beautiful as a movie star, with her styled blond hair framing that amazingly lovely face—which helped well with the photos she included with her articles, or so she'd indicated.

He took a step toward her where she still stood near the sink. He had an urge to take her into his arms.

They'd be alone for a while tonight, after all. In his condo. Even though she had a separate bedroom.

But although she smiled at him, she moved away. Not toward that bedroom. She looked down at Lorrie. "Before I get started on the computer though, I want to take Lorrie out for a quick walk."

She had already fed her dog a dinner of canned dog food that appeared to be a healthy brand, from what he'd heard in discussions at Barky Boulevard by the staff and people who brought their pets in.

He wasn't surprised Harper did the right thing about that too. Especially when it came to caring for the dog she clearly loved, who'd not been around for their earlier relationship. He wondered when Harper had acquired Lorrie. The dog didn't appear to be a puppy now, so he figured Lorrie might have been brought into Harper's family as a substitute for his company when their relationship had ended.

He would have to ask her sometime.

For now, he said, "I'd enjoy accompanying both of you on that walk."

And keeping an eye on their surroundings.

To make sure Harper remained safe.

Chapter 8

Okay. Harper was soon alone in her guest bedroom with the door closed. A little lonesome already? Maybe, although Lorrie was with her, of course. And she had things to do—starting with checking her email.

The room was small, too small for a desk or even a bureau, though there were some shelves in the closet where she could stack the clothes that she didn't hang up. But there was no place she could put her computer while she worked.

Except on her lap as she sat on the blue, fluffy comforter on the queen-sized bed, with Lorrie lying on the floor beside her.

That was fine. She'd written on her laptop in a lot of places over the years, so she would just do it again here.

Bryson had given her the password for his condo's Wi-Fi, so after she turned her computer on she was able to quickly get onto the internet.

And she drew in her breath before she opened her email.

Nothing immediately stood out as containing more threats. She noted the addresses of a couple of her primary editors, and hopefully all was okay there. And there were a lot more.

First thing, she did as promised and sent links to a few of her favorite, older, noncontroversial articles to Kara Province.

Then it was time to check her emails.

A few were from Wanda, the editor she wanted to contact the most at the moment. But she'd wait to look at them when she'd done some initial checking about her recent article for *Pup Rescue Forever*

She did see Macie's address, and she opened that email first.

Where are you, Harper? it asked. Are you okay? Did you get the latest series of threats I received here— threats against you from an unnamed source—again? Possibly the same source, although the address wasn't familiar.

Harper swallowed hard. The email was short. Macie hadn't included whatever the threats said.

But Harper had to assume that, with the mention, these were new threats. Did they indicate any further who was sending them? Why? Whether the person had any idea where Harper was?

And why send them to Macie and not Harper? Although… Well, she didn't recognize some of the senders of the emails she'd received today, though she assumed some could be from fans, since she did hear from quite a few of them. That certainly would be welcome. And others could be ads or spam that hadn't automatically gone into her spam file.

But was that it?

Could they be some of the threats Macie had told her about?

She would check…eventually.

She would also have to get in touch with Macie later, again by email.

As difficult as that would be.

And it was also difficult to simply ignore—sort of—Macie's current email letting her know she was under threat yet again.

But next, even before looking at those emails she had received from unknown senders in case any contained threats, she decided to check any reviews and pans of her latest *Pup Rescue Forever* article online before she even started drafting her email to Wanda.

Theoretically, she could have checked them out on her phone while she had no access to her computer. But she would have wanted to be alone for that, and she'd had very little alone time since her conversation with Macie. A restroom stop, yes, but she'd needed to get back to her work as Hanna at Barky as soon as possible and wanted to be able to really read those reviews Macie had mentioned. And if they were as bad as Macie had indicated, joining other people she needed to impress for now, like Andrea and the Barky Boulevard employees, wouldn't have been good if she'd gotten upset.

Even more so with Bryson, although she'd be up front about them if they discussed them here.

So now, she would check out reviews for her article about Pet Me For Life Shelter in Pasadena—apparently at least some critical ones. But it was a shelter she really liked. One where she had gone several times, spoken with the manager and assistant managers, seen how they treated the dogs and cats cared for there. She'd taken photographs. And then she had written her story.

Oh, she had included some not-so-great areas at the

shelter in those photos. Shown how a few dogs were sniffing around, possibly eating trash or other things they shouldn't inside large enclosures. At least the dogs weren't always confined in small cages. But it was a shelter, and the staff and volunteers couldn't be everywhere there, any more than they were at other similar, caring shelters.

And as she'd been leaving one of the first times, she had seen a person coming in with an apparent Chihuahua mix. She'd spoken with that person briefly and been told that the dog had recently been adopted from Pet Me For Life, and there'd been some behavioral problems so she was being returned, apparently not adapting well to the home's children, or to complete housebreaking.

Harper had taken that dog's picture too, and asked about her on her next visit. The manager had indicated that the problem was more about the former adopter than the poor dog who'd been brought back, and still not rehomed.

It was an interesting, somewhat sad story, and Harper had included it in her article. She always liked to tell the truth, what she saw and not what she felt, and rarely criticized the people or shelters. She was proud of being a journalist, not especially an op-ed writer, so she told things that she learned about without analyzing them too deeply.

Did the criticisms have something to do with that? Well, she'd find out.

She did a Google search about *Pup Rescue Forever* article reviews. She had called her article "Pet Me For Life Today, Tomorrow and Forever," and a few references to reviews about it did begin to show up.

The first one she saw, on the Facebook account of someone she recognized as providing a lot of reviews for her stories, was a good one, which wasn't surprising, since that person apparently liked what Harper wrote about and always shared positive reviews in previous posts.

The next one she saw though—not so good. Possibly one of those Macie had been referring to when she mentioned the issues to Harper. In fact, that person, on X/Twitter, really jumped on Harper's article, slamming the fact that it didn't dive into how awful the shelter really was, considering the way it handled the dog who'd been returned there and the terrible person who'd done the returning. Even worse, the post was highly critical of Harper herself for not doing more to learn about, and fix, the situation for the poor dog. And other dogs at that shelter who might also get returned from their adoptions. Did Harper even check on that?

That post had a lot of comments. And the person who did the posting? It was a woman Harper had never heard of before, and when she used her own X/Twitter account to try to check on that woman, she found that there were hardly any other posts by her except ones regarding Harper's story, but those apparently continued to get lots of views and comments, many also indicating criticism of Harper and her story.

Had that person created that account especially for that purpose? Maybe, but even if that was true what could Harper do about it?

Nothing for now. But it hurt to see those nasty criticisms that were sometimes questioned and sometimes agreed with by readers. And that reviewer also criticized not only Harper herself, but also mentioned that she wrote other articles involving animal shelters and pets, and that she didn't always tell the truth in them.

But those were lies, not her stories.

Still, all she could do was sigh.

There was no way to fix that review or its comments. And unfortunately, some of those comments also included bad reviews of the article, with those who'd posted them indicating they had read it and also had major problems with it.

Harper figured she could step up and respond to the review and other nasty posts, but that wouldn't get her anywhere.

Criticisms like this were partially what had sent her here to Chance—since some contained threats too.

Not these, at least. But she couldn't help but suspect that the person who posted the underlying review might be the same one, or was allied with, whoever had been threatening her. Maybe some of the commenters too.

And despite the fact that she often received a lot of good reviews along with the bad, it appeared that no one except the first poster had said nice things about the article.

Maybe no one else wanted to do anything the nasty poster might consider confrontational.

Or could that person have found a way to delete any other good reviews?

Harper could hope that was the case, and that there had been other people who had liked this story, which should not have been considered so controversial.

But she might never know.

And for the moment, what she wanted to do was contact Wanda, apologize despite not being able to fix the situation—and learn if Wanda knew anything else.

She looked through her emails and located the first few from Wanda about the article. Happily, the editor had apparently really liked it, at least at first, and sent Harper an online free link to the issue of *Pup Rescue Forever* where it was being published.

Harper couldn't help smiling. And then she figured, as much as she would like to respond to that one, she needed to see Wanda's correspondence sent after the bad review and its disapproving comments had started showing up.

She saw four more from Wanda. Harper closed her eyes briefly, then clicked to open each one in order.

At first, Wanda had just seemed unhappy to see the bad review and some of its comments. Then she asked Harper how much research she had done. Was the Pet Me For Life Shelter really as kind and caring as Harper had written? If so, why had the nasty criticisms been in that review? Yes, there appeared to be only one reviewer doing that, but a lot of readers had apparently agreed with the review. Word was now out there that the shelter treated its animals cruelly…and the nice compliments in the article written by Harper Morsley were entirely fabricated. The review even said the shelter might have paid Harper to lie and be kind—and Wanda wanted to know if that was true.

Which, of course, it wasn't. Now that she had seen Wanda's increasingly upset and critical emails, Harper would let her know.

If only she could also identify the reviewer and give a logical explanation why the person had lied so nastily.

And out there in public, criticizing not only Harper, but also *Pup Rescue Forever* for including such an allegedly false story.

She could only hope the shelter itself hadn't been affected badly by all of this. It did save animals, after all.

Okay. Time to respond to Wanda. Although not exactly.

Her preference would have been to send a reply to Wanda's first, complimentary email, but she didn't want the editor to think she hadn't seen the bad review or the comments about it, or Wanda's emails regarding the bad review and comments.

Neither did she want to reply directly to any of Wanda's more recent and more difficult communications.

Therefore, she started a new email, where she thanked the editor for her initial comments and said she had seen the highly critical review and the posted responses, good and bad, as well as Wanda's resulting emails to her.

I can't say for sure, she ended, but I wouldn't be surprised if whoever posted that nasty review is the same person who'd been posting at least some of the other bad reviews of my work and sending me threats. Have you received any mentioning me, btw? In any case, please be assured that I did my homework on this article as I always do. I was favorably impressed with the Pet Me For Life Shelter as I'd indicated, as well as their taking that poor dog who was the subject of the criticism back and caring for it once more. Harper stopped and reread what she'd written, then added at the end, And in case you're wondering, I am currently researching another possible article for Pup Rescue Forever about another shelter.

Which wasn't exactly true, although she was always researching animal shelters, and she'd be doing more soon, remotely, of course.

And, hopefully, getting to see what the Chance Animal Shelter was really like. But as she'd promised, she would only submit articles about it for publication that she had gotten okayed by Scott.

Scott, whom she hoped to see tomorrow and sell her own predicament to.

Now, she reread again her email to Wanda, added some niceties encouraging the editor to let her know if there was any article subject matter she'd like to see soon from Harper, then clicked Send.

And hoped Wanda's response would be positive, so Harper could continue to submit to that publication in the future despite the current nastiness.

Which she would try to figure out as soon as she could, and try to determine who'd written and posted that nasty review and encouraged the equally nasty comments.

For now, she would read her additional emails, most likely delete them after making sure those from addresses she didn't recognize were spam or otherwise nothing she'd want to respond to.

One turned out to be simply an ad for an online research resource for writers that charged a lot.

The next was from a fan whose name she didn't recognize, but the woman said she lived in Baltimore and volunteered at a pet shelter there and very much enjoyed Harper's articles about other shelters all over the country, both good and bad.

If she'd read the story about Pet Me For Life and the

bad review and comments, she didn't mention it. The email had been sent last night, so all of that would most likely have been visible to the sender, so maybe she had seen it and decided to write directly to Harper at the email address on her website in support of the journalist.

Which Harper appreciated, whether or not that was the reason for the woman's kind communication.

She sent a thank-you response and wished she could tell where her next article would appear, but she didn't currently have anything scheduled. She smiled and sighed as she sent that one off.

She opened the next one. And gasped.

It said, Haven't you stopped all that writing yet? Some is good. Too much, and for the wrong publications, is not. And I know where you are and how to stop you forever.

Okay, maybe he was overly concerned. Overly protective.

But Bryson kept finding reasons to be in his hallway that evening, walking slowly by the closed door to the guest bedroom. He figured he'd better have a reason to claim he was there in case Harper opened the door, maybe to take Lorrie out or for some other purpose. But he needed to know she was inside, and that she remained safe in his home, as she had at Barky Boulevard.

He'd passed by several times. This was at least the sixth.

And this time he heard something from inside, a soft cry from Harper.

Was she talking to her dog? Didn't seem like it. Not unless Lorrie was misbehaving.

Surely the dog wasn't hurt.

But rational or not, Bryson had to go inside and check it out.

He paused to knock. Even though this was his condo, and Harper was his guest and entitled to her privacy, he still had an urge to push the door open and hurry in to learn what was going on, assuming that noise had meant something was wrong.

As he put his hand on the doorknob, though, the door was pulled open. Harper stood there. The expression on her attractive face suggested horror.

"Harper, what's wrong?" he began, but instead of just answering, Harper surged into his arms.

He hugged her close, feeling her shake. Heard her crying softly.

But not answering his question.

Not for a minute or so. But then she stepped back. "I… I want to show you something," she said in a trembling voice.

He could guess what, and he was right.

Lorrie had come out with her, and now the little dog snuggled against her person's legs, clearly showing concern. Sweet pup, Bryson thought.

He followed Harper back into the guest bedroom. He wasn't surprised to see her laptop open on top of the bed.

She motioned for him to follow, then sit down. She moved the computer around so he could see the screen.

As he had figured, she had an open email there, and he read the threat.

And the claim the menace knew where Harper was.

Bryson hoped not. That person might say anything

to scare his target and possibly get her to reveal her location, which they most likely didn't know.

"Okay," he said grimly. "I believe that jerk is lying, but we can't be sure. I'm glad we're going to take you to the Chance Animal Shelter tomorrow and talk to Scott."

An odd—ridiculous?—thought suddenly shot through him. Could Harper have sent this to herself so she could show it to Scott and use it to get him to allow her to stay?

He'd already considered that Harper could be a good actress at times, based on what he had seen of her in their past together. Might she be reacting this way, in apparent terror, as a good performance?

Anything was possible, but he wanted to believe her. He *did* believe her.

And he wanted to soothe her as well as keep her safe.

"I'm definitely glad too," she said. "But do I dare hope that Scott will allow me to stay? I mean, I want to show him this email. But if he's dead set against letting me move in there because of my journalism career, he can claim I sent it to myself. Made up everything, including the nasty review I got of my latest article that's gotten me a lot of online criticism. No threats there, but it's similar enough to reviews in the past that seemed involved with the threatening communications that brought me here." She let go of him, backed away and looked straight at him with her clearly pained green eyes. "I'm scared, Bryson. And—"

"That's not surprising," he told her, stepping close again. "I'm going to call Kara, tell her what's going on, ask her to step up the patrols around here tonight. I'll also contact Scott and tell him we'll be at the shelter first thing in the morning. And meantime, tonight—"

He pulled her into his arms. "I want you to sleep in bed with me. Nothing sexual or anything like that." Although the idea of sleeping with her again that way did turn him on, even now. But coming on to her under these circumstances would be way out of line. "That way I can make sure you're safe tonight."

She seemed to be holding him close too. But what was she thinking?

She drew slightly away and looked at him again. "Thank you, Bryson," she said. She reached up, pulled his head down…and kissed him. Briefly. Not sensually, even though his already hard body part grew even harder at the feel of her lips on his.

He returned that kiss, also keeping it more caring than heated, then stepped back.

"You're welcome," he said. "Now, it's nearly bedtime. I'll make a couple of phone calls, and once I find out from Kara when the next patrol will be around here, we'll take Lorrie for a short walk around the center courtyard, and head to bed after that. I still have some of my law-enforcement weapons around and I'll make sure they're accessible quickly, though I doubt I'll need them. But you can be certain I'll be there for you, Harper."

He moved toward her once more and kissed her again.

And she definitely participated.

Chapter 9

Maybe she shouldn't feel any more at ease than she did an hour or so ago when she'd seen that threatening email, panicked and started running out the bedroom door to find Bryson.

What could he have done about it, after all?

But he had done exactly what she had hoped for that moment—taken her into his arms, promised to get even more law-enforcement patrols around his place, stay with her and watch over her more…and even take care of her in person that night.

By having her sleep in his room with him.

Which was where she was now.

They hadn't gone to bed right away. First, they sat in his living room together while he called Kara Province on her private number, which she had given him, put the call on his phone's speaker and told her what was going on. It was late enough that Kara indicated she wasn't at the station, but she was kind enough to sound concerned, and promised she would call in right away to get even more patrols in the area.

"Just so you know," she added, "whether or not you've seen them, we already have quite a few marked cars driving around there and some unmarked too. There were more around Barky Boulevard before too, during the day, and will be again tomorrow." She paused. "Glad you two let me know about this additional threat. The Chance PD wants to be informed about anything that could harm anyone in the area, civilians or otherwise, and we'll do all we can to prevent anyone from being hurt."

"I understand that from talking with both Sherm and you," Bryson said, "and appreciate it."

"And I really appreciate all you are doing too." Harper knew what she'd said sounded heartfelt, which it was.

"Oh, and by the way, Harper, thanks for sending those links to your articles," Kara said. "I look forward to reading them when I have a chance. And I have a temporary license plate for you that I'll leave in a sealed envelope at Barky Boulevard."

They'd waited for maybe half an hour until Kara called back and assured them the additional patrols had begun. Only then did Bryson allow Harper to take Lorrie outside, into the condo's courtyard, with him accompanying them.

Lorrie hadn't taken long to accomplish what she'd needed to, and soon they were all back inside Bryson's unit.

Harper and he took turns showering for the night. Now, Harper had on some comfortable but fortunately not particularly sexy pink-and-white pj's.

They were lying in his comfortable, firm queen-sized bed together, beneath the beige sheets, warm brown blanket and plaid comforter. And the idea wasn't for their prior relationship to get in the way here. Harper recognized that. Bryson had said he'd feel more confident in watching over her if he was doing exactly that—keeping watch around her environment. And that could only happen when they were together.

Which meant they shared a bed, as they had often a few years ago.

But unlike then, there was nothing physical between them. There couldn't be.

Yet Harper couldn't help but be well aware of Bryson's presence beside her. His warm, muscular body, also wearing not especially sexy pj's—blue ones. He was still quite obviously there. Not close. Not now.

Although they had shared a couple of brief kisses when they'd settled into bed, as they had earlier, before bedtime. Which probably hadn't been a good idea, since it only made Harper much more aware of how sexy Bryson still was.

How appealing.

And how much her body yearned to get even closer, share more than the bed, but some touches—and more—too.

Very bad idea, and not just because they no longer had a relationship. After all, she shouldn't do anything that might distract him from staying aware of their surroundings, making sure that this cop in doggy day care clothing during the day remained alert and watchful and listening for any possible threat to her nearby.

And so, she just lay there in the near darkness, except for a small night-light near the lower side of the closet door, listening to Lorrie's slight snoring from the dog bed near Harper on the floor. Listening to hear whether Bryson was snoring too, which he wasn't. As she recalled, he seldom had when they'd been together, although she was often aware of his deep breathing while he was asleep and she had lain awake beside him.

In those days, she had simply enjoyed his presence, often after making love at least once. Wondered how long they'd get to stay together at night, since she sometimes had to hurry away to other areas the following days to research her stories.

Wondered if that would be a long-term, possibly lifetime routine…but it hadn't been.

And now, they were together for a far different reason, even though Harper couldn't help wishing things were closer to how they had been in the past.

After all, she might feel better to think they had a potential relationship brewing again rather than him only being his cop self and hanging out with a person in trouble.

Her.

She felt herself sigh at the thought, but at least she kept it quiet.

But Bryson was clearly awake too.

"You okay, Harper?"

She wanted to sigh again at her own folly that had apparently disturbed him. Or maybe he had been hoping she was awake too so they could talk some more.

Was that a good idea?

For now, she simply responded, "I'm fine."

"But I assume you're thinking, right."

"I'm always thinking." She attempted to sound droll.

"Except when you're asleep, I assume," he said. "Your thinking then would simply be dreams."

"Who says my dreams are simple?"

He laughed, and she felt the bed beside her shake

slightly. "Got it." He paused, then said, "If you want to talk about what's going on, or anything else, it doesn't matter what time it is. I'm here for you."

That was sweet of him to say, although she already knew it was true.

"Thank you," she said softly. "I just wish—" She hesitated.

"Wish what? Although I can guess."

She felt the bed move again, and suddenly Bryson, lying on his side under the blankets, was right beside her.

"I'd like to say I wish none of this was happening," she said. "Only—"

"Only?" he prompted again.

Was it wise to say what was on her mind? Probably not, and she'd have to clarify it.

"Only," she continued after a moment, "if none of this was happening, I'm sure I wouldn't be seeing you now." She hesitated. "Oh, I don't mean that I'm thinking anything is going to happen between us again. I know better. But, well, I can't help appreciating the way you stepped up to help me when you saw me and recognized I have a problem. It's—it's so nice to have such a kind and caring friend."

And friendship of sorts was all there was between them now. Nothing more. Not ever again.

Bryson remained silent at first, although Harper was pleased when he moved even closer and put his arms around her. She snuggled against him, her head against his hard chest.

Then he said, "I never stopped thinking about you, Harper. Oh, I don't mean you were on my mind every moment, but when I saw magazines and newspapers in stores or wherever, especially those that clearly were about animals, I thought about you, even when I didn't see stories you wrote."

She'd thought about him often too. Too often. But how much should she reveal?

She had to say something. "I wondered about you a lot too. I assumed you remained in the Los Angeles Police Department and kept an eye open about things that were going on in the area with law enforcement…and when someone was injured." Or worse.

Not that she'd wished that on him. Quite the contrary.

It shouldn't have mattered after their breakup, especially not after the way he had hurt her, but she definitely wanted him to remain alive and unharmed.

And being a journalist, she'd kept a close watch on the media to make sure he never appeared to be the subject of a story—injured, or harming anyone else and therefore getting in the public eye as a possible over-zealous cop.

She'd not kept in touch with anyone who'd been friends of both of them, so she couldn't check on him that way. And even though she knew he cared about animals and kept an eye on rescue organizations, that didn't seem to be a good way to keep track of him either.

"Well, fortunately, while I was still an active cop I managed to do my job without being too obvious about it, except to others on the force and my superiors. And even more fortunately, I was never hurt. But I did manage to help bring down some pretty nasty crooks, or *accused* crooks. And you'll be interested to hear that I arrested some of them for cruelty to animals, both at alleged rescue organizations and otherwise."

"That sounds like you," she said softly, and snuggled against him more.

His arms tightened around her, and she allowed herself to close her eyes as she lay with him in his bed, being protected by him, being *with* him.

And soon, after making herself listen for any irregular noises, and hearing none she recognized, she was finally falling asleep.

When Harper started breathing more deeply in his arms, Bryson just lay there, holding her close but not too tightly, loving the feel of her yet experiencing mixed emotions about being here with her that way.

Her curves, her warmth against him, stirred memories he had long since cast aside, or at least tried to.

But even though there shouldn't be anything sexy— or too sexy—about having her sleeping so near, he realized he wanted her. Again. Possibly still.

After all, he had never completely forgotten about her, although for those years apart he had sort of convinced himself he was better off without her.

That intelligent, smart-mouthed, opinionated woman who had become so angry when he had dared to criticize one of the things she had written, partially because she had dared to criticize other cops for doing their jobs in helping to protect people and, somewhat, animals.

Although he did admit to himself afterward that the police department in question had seemed a bit too zealous in wanting to get stray dogs rounded up in their neighborhoods, and not just sticking them then in shelters that would find ways to keep them alive and get them rehomed. And—

Okay, he was overthinking this, when he should be paying more attention to listening to what was around them.

Like the sound of Harper's breathing in his arms, yes, despite how her closeness continued to rouse one of his body parts.

And her dog's breathing on the floor beside them. The little French bulldog had a flat nose, which probably made it harder for Lorrie to breathe, and so she actually snored a bit.

And beyond them? He heard a few cars go by on the road outside, and an airplane or two overhead. A dog barking in the distance.

Nothing alarming.

But would he, could he, hear it if anyone was attempting to get onto the condo property and into his condo? He would certainly do all he could to listen, and watch, for anything out of the ordinary.

Right now, he had an urge to slip away from Harper, out of his bed, stick on some clothes and do a quick patrol around the area.

But was it realistic to think that whoever was after her actually knew not only that she was in Chance, but also that she was here, staying with him?

Who knew? He just wished he knew who it was, and his mind kept churning out possibilities.

From all she had said, the only suspects he could come up with were other writers who were jealous of her success and wanted her to stop writing. Maybe they just wanted to frighten her.

But journalists as killers? And just because they were jealous?

Well, he couldn't rule them out, but he didn't really think that made sense. Unless those journalists had some other reason to dislike Harper, of course.

Okay, he finally thought. Enough of this.

If he didn't get some sleep, how would he be able to protect her in the morning?

Although they planned on going to the Chance Animal Shelter, which was well protected, thanks to Scott Sherridan and all he had done to make the place secure and keep it that way.

And as much as Bryson liked having Harper in his condo, so close to him, and at Barky Boulevard during the day, he would do what he could to help convince Scott to accept her. And keep her safe with the "staff members" there, those people under the shelter's protection.

But he had to be lucid when they arrived there. So time to get some sleep.

Only…he felt Harper move in his arms.

Had she been breathing as deeply over the past few minutes when his thoughts had raced around that way?

"Bryson?" Her voice was soft and sleepy, but clearly she was now awake. "Is everything okay?"

"Sure," he said.

"You've been awake making sure it is." She moved even more, sitting up now. "I appreciate it, but, really, you need to get some sleep too. Maybe I should just go back to the guest bedroom and—"

"No, you should stay here," he said. "I've no reason to think there's anything going on around this condo, except that I'm a cop and that's my job—worrying. And—"

"And doing your damnedest to keep me safe at the

moment." Her expression, visible in the faint glow from the night-light, appeared grateful. And caring.

And he did exactly what he knew he shouldn't, especially now, while he was trying to make sure there were no dangers around them. Around *her*.

He edged closer to her, also sitting up. And put his arms around her again.

And kissed her, wondering if she was awake enough to kiss him back.

Or whether she would want to...

Oh, yeah. This kiss was a lot more than those few they'd shared since they'd come into each other's presence again.

Maybe partially due to being still in bed, maybe only half-awake, not necessarily awake enough to consider the consequences.

Or at least that was Bryson's excuse to himself.

And instead of attempting to find a comfortable way for them to sit there on the bed while they kissed, Bryson gently maneuvered them both so they were lying down again. Facing each other. Arms around each other.

And, yes, sharing a kiss that grew more and more heated as he moved his head around on Harper's pillow, then moved so his head was over hers.

How he enjoyed the feel of Harper's warm, searching lips on his. The way he was able to play with her tongue with his, and she teased him back with hers, in a way that suggested she wanted more than a kiss... Felt like the thrusting movements they might engage in should they begin to have sex together.

And the way that certain body part of his, which had already been hardening a lot in Harper's presence the closer they got, made it clearer that he should definitely consider engaging in some activity to utilize it in the way it suggested even more now.

He moved on top of her, feeling her delicious upper curves against him through her pj's, and also feeling what seemed like growing heat below—and not just his.

Was he being too aggressive? Too presumptuous?

He definitely hoped not, but—

"Harper," he began. "If this isn't okay with you, I'll—"

"Don't tell me you're going to stop," she rasped, throwing her arms around him and thrusting her lower body against him, against his erection that seemed to be hardening and growing even more, if that was possible.

"I'm not stopping unless you want me to," he said through clenched teeth.

"I don't want you to," she responded, and reached down to start pulling off his pajama bottoms.

Chapter 10

Oh, my. Oh, yes!

Harper knew this wasn't a good idea…but it was the best idea. It wasn't what she'd had in mind before… maybe. But now it was exactly what she had in mind.

She'd already considered making love with Bryson again despite their differences, and all the time they'd been apart.

But she knew better, and she'd even told Bryson that a while earlier.

Now though… Well, right or wrong, foolish or smart, they'd started. She continued to pull his pajama bottoms down until she was able to not just feel him against her, but also see, in the dim light, his wonderful erection.

She drew in her breath even as she reached down to grasp it, and heard Bryson gasp too, even as he began to touch her breasts beneath her pajama top.

She heard a sound beside them but realized right away it wasn't someone trying to get in and harm either of them.

Without releasing Bryson, or moving far enough away to stop him from touching her, she rolled over slightly and looked toward the floor beside the bed.

"It's okay, Lorrie," she told her dog, who'd evidently

been awakened by the movements and sounds above her. "Go back to sleep."

That wasn't a command she had taught Lorrie, but apparently the calmness of her tone must have meant something to the pup since Harper didn't hear any further stirring.

Or maybe she was just too focused on the way Bryson, after laughing slightly, continued to gently massage her sensitive and stimulated breasts.

And as she moaned, his hands moved lower, as she continued to stroke him.

She wasn't sure who moved next, but soon Bryson pulled away, ever so slightly, and somehow a condom magically appeared in his hand. He must have kept one nearby. Or put one under his pillow or mattress or wherever, just in case. And then, after quickly putting it on, he was on top of her, inside her, moving and thrusting, as she also thrust her hips upward to encourage him.

And she reveled in their lovemaking, even allowing herself to think briefly about its familiarity, and how wonderful it had been before…and how it was even more wonderful now.

Then she cried out as she reached satisfaction, and heard Bryson moan loudly too, suggesting he had also climaxed, a familiar moan she recalled from their past.

And her orgasm too had been familiar. Only…was it possible this one was even more satisfying than the others she'd experienced before?

Or was it—

Like everything else around this wonderful man, she was overthinking this.

She needed to remain in the present.

And in the present, she had just had one of the more memorable experiences in her life.

For now, she remained in his arms, breathing loudly, his heated body on top of hers as he also breathed deeply and continued to hold her.

"Oh, Bryson," she said softly.

He didn't respond vocally but pressed his mouth down on hers again, and kissed her, not as heatedly as before but with care.

And she responded similarly, in thanks and with happiness, as they wound down.

Soon they were lying there, still in each other's arms, no longer moving despite how their bodies remained warm and together.

"Wow," Bryson said, his voice low. "Even better than I remembered, which was damned good."

"Ditto from my perspective," she responded, as she snuggled her head against his chest even more.

She was satisfied. She was sated.

She was exhausted. And yet did she dare sleep?

The reason for her being here in the first place insinuated itself inside her head.

It must have been obvious to Bryson. Or maybe he had started thinking about it too, now that they were finished.

For now.

But she didn't dare to think about any more.

And somehow, she finally started to fall asleep, still cuddled in Bryson's gentle grip that seemed to become even more firm and soothing. Maybe that was why she was able to relax. And sleep.

She wasn't aware of anything else for a long while until a bit of movement on the floor beside her—beside *them*—woke her. Bryson was no longer holding her, but he remained snug against her, breathing in the same cadence she recalled from the past, noticeable but no snoring.

She figured Lorrie had stirred, but she didn't stand up on her hind legs and lean against the mattress, which would indicate she needed to go outside, although Harper realized she would need to take the pup out soon.

For now though, she just lay there, still enjoying the warmth of the muscular man beside her. Against her.

Even though he was asleep, she still felt protected by his strong presence. She listened to their surroundings though, and heard nothing besides her still-stirring pup, and Bryson's breathing.

She thought about the day ahead, and what was likely to occur. They would head for the Chance Animal Shelter, where she would get her opportunity to try to finally convince Scott Sherridan that she was really being threatened by someone unknown and needed protection.

Protection beyond what Bryson could provide, since as much as she worried about herself, she now worried about him too, and whatever the menacing person after her might try if they ever found out about Bryson.

At least the shelter was apparently all about taking care of people they accepted to live there. From what she gathered, Scott remained a local undercover cop. And, well, she would hopefully learn more today about the shelter's environment and how it worked.

It was an environment that would remain in her mind and not appear on her computer screen, no matter how tempted she became to write about it, as she did about so many other things involving animals. She'd promised, and it made sense.

And—

"You're awake." Bryson's clear voice made it obvious he was too.

"So are you. So should we get the day started? I'll want to get dressed right away and take Lorrie out." And hope that Bryson would join them, although she wouldn't mention that.

He did though. "Sure, let's go. I figured that the pup would need to take care of business soon, now that she's awake. I heard her moving, although she's obviously a good girl and didn't disturb either of us."

"Oh, yes, she's a good girl."

Harper began getting out of bed, but stopped and turned back toward Bryson. Crawling slightly toward him, she gave him a quick, nonsuggestive kiss. And only then did she pull the covers completely off, turn and put her feet on the floor. She was still without clothes, but would fix that soon. And she was delighted that she didn't feel even a tiny bit embarrassed about remaining naked near Bryson.

Of course, he still was naked too. She noticed that as he began getting out of bed on the other side, and tamped down the urge to go touch him again. Not now, certainly.

And really, despite how enjoyable last night had been, it was most likely an aberration. After all, Bryson wouldn't be with her other nights if her wishes came true and she was accepted at the Chance Animal Shelter.

She wasn't surprised when Lorrie came over and stood on her hind legs against the bed, wagging her behind and clearly happy she now had attention. Harper went over to the nearby chair, where she had left the clothes she had worn yesterday, and started dressing. Her suitcase and backpacks that contained additional clothing remained in the guest bedroom. She'd change into something else later, after taking Lorrie out and before they left to go to the shelter. She figured Bryson would understand and not be grossed out by her putting on the same stuff she'd had on before. And if he was, he didn't say anything.

In moments, she was ready, and turned back and saw that Bryson was too. He also wore what he'd had on yesterday. To make her feel better? Or was that mostly the same thing he wore to Barky Boulevard each day?

For he would undoubtedly go there later, hopefully leaving her at the Chance Animal Shelter, although there was always the possibility she'd be returning there too, if Scott rejected her.

"Ready to go out?" Bryson asked her. Lorrie must have understood the gist of what he was saying, since she hurried over to him and began wagging her behind as if saying "yes."

The three of them went through the bedroom door and down the hall to the condo's main entry. But Bryson gestured for Harper and Lorrie to wait while he went outside into the hallway first.

Which only increased Harper's appreciation of this kind, protective old friend. The friend and more she had slept with last night…

She had to stop thinking about that, as much as she'd enjoyed it. It was behind her, behind *them*, now. She had the rest of her life to consider.

But would they talk about it?

Well, she'd most likely not bring it up, but who knew?

Bryson returned. "I didn't expect anything out there would seem off, and it doesn't. But we'll still be cautious."

Which they were, getting on the elevator that arrived quickly and took them down to the lobby with Bryson preceding them once more.

A few people were there, so Bryson took charge of watching over Harper, saying hello to a couple he knew, which seemed okay. And he didn't appear overly concerned about those he didn't greet, since they were friendly too, making over Lorrie. Apparently dogs were welcome in the building, or at least these people seemed to welcome Lorrie.

They took Lorrie out through the door that led to the yard in the building's center, as before. And as before, Harper's smart and wonderful dog did what she needed to fast, and Harper dealt with it.

Back inside shortly after that, Bryson told Harper he'd make them a quick breakfast. He'd done that often in the past. He did breakfast, and she generally took care of dinner.

She had left Lorrie's bowl and food in the kitchen, so first thing she did was get her pup's breakfast together, as well as make sure the other bowl on the floor had water in it. Lorrie seemed happy as she began to eat.

Harper wasn't surprised that Bryson quickly prepared scrambled eggs, fried potatoes and wheat toast, as well as coffee from one of those coffee makers that used pods. She chose one with a hint of hazelnut in it.

And while she waited, Harper tried hard not to think about how she would approach Scott. She'd wing it, but tell him the truth, of course.

Including about those latest threats.

She had an urge to get on her computer while waiting, just to see if there was anything else. Instead, she took a quick look at her phone, which she'd stuck in her pocket. Fortunately, she had remembered to charge last night.

Yes, she had gotten a few emails—one from Wanda, another from Macie and a third from Betsy Bordley, her third primary editor. They all just seemed to be checking in with her without mentioning any problems, only asking if she had any new articles in the works. Not even Macie mentioned any threats this time, and Wanda didn't bring up the bad-review issue. Had things calmed down, or were the editors simply tired of mentioning problems?

Harper also heard from a few other editors and fans, plus some spam. Nothing appeared at all menacing. Could the threats be over?

She could hardly count on it.

And, tensing up, she checked to see if the ones from yesterday were still there. They were, since she hadn't deleted them, and because she could also access them on her phone she didn't have to count on the ability to use a computer while she was arguing her case to Scott.

If only she didn't have to...

"You okay?" Bryson's voice was sharp as he brought her cup of coffee to her at the table. "Did you see any new emails or—"

"Some new but nothing threatening," she said, attempting to sound happy. And in a way she was. "Is breakfast ready?" She'd been so wrapped up in checking her phone that she hadn't been paying attention to what Bryson was doing, or his progress.

"Yeah, but are you sure you want to eat? We could just head to the shelter now, and eat this stuff on the way."

"I want to eat now," she said firmly. "Here." She paused. "You're right that I want to head to the shelter soon, but breakfast here is fine."

She hoped. She had no reason to think that whoever was threatening her was on the way to this location, so no immediate departure was necessary.

A quick one after eating, though, seemed like a good idea.

Right now, she took a sip of her hot, tasty coffee, then rose as Bryson prepared to dish out their breakfast.

She would enjoy it as much as she could, especially considering the fact that, if all went well, this would likely be the last meal she would share with Bryson in his condo.

Bryson, finished cooking, now sat at the table across from Harper. He was glad he had been able to put this meal together for them, he thought as he sat down after dishing some eggs, skillet-fried potatoes and a piece of toast onto their plates and they both started eating.

They'd eat, then leave. He'd make quick calls to Kara and Scott when they were on their way—Kara, to make sure she knew they'd be out and about so the nearest patrols could keep an eye on them, and Scott, so he would expect them, and be ready to talk with Harper.

And hopefully do as Harper, and Bryson too, wanted: accept her into the Chance Animal Shelter, at least for now, while Bryson, in cooperation with the Chance PD, would spend more time trying to figure out who was threatening Harper and why...and find a way to get whoever it was into custody so the threats would stop.

The good thing about this situation was that he was thinking like a cop again.

As much as he loved his aunt, and enjoyed helping her run her doggy day care place, including playing with dogs, he wanted to go back to his real life as a cop in LA.

Or at least that was what he had wanted until Harper had barged back into his world. For the moment he would do all he could, cop or not, to protect her. And when things returned to normal for her again, which they eventually would, she would go back to her own life, he figured, and maybe he'd be able to do the same by then.

For now, they chatted as though nothing was on their minds but their food and Barky and life in general.

Neither brought up what they would soon be doing: heading for the shelter, pleading her case to Scott.

And, of course, Bryson had mixed feelings about whether he really wanted Harper to wind up staying behind those walls for any length of time.

He only hoped he, and the Chance PD, and maybe Scott as well, would be able to pin down the source of those threats and make sure whoever sent them was dealt with appropriately.

"Everything okay?" Harper was looking at him, a forkful of egg near her mouth, her expression full of concern.

"Just thinking too much," he told her.

"I can identify with that," she said. "Meanwhile... I really like our breakfast. But I'm pretty much done."

"Me too."

Bryson took a few more sips of his coffee to finish

it, and saw Harper eat her last bites of toast, then also take a final drink of coffee.

She rose immediately to pick up the plates and cups and take them to the sink, which had been what she had done in the past when they had eaten too, as well as last night after their pizza dinner. He pretended to forget that she hadn't allowed him to help much before, and started to place the plates and flatware in the dishwasher. There weren't any leftovers for him to pack up and stick in the fridge this morning.

"You don't remember the old routine," she said, sounding exasperated.

"Oh, I do. But it is old, as you said. And we need to get going soon."

She laughed and nodded. "I agree. Thanks."

It didn't take long to finish what little organizing needed to be done in the kitchen, both of them working together that way.

And Bryson liked their mutual cooperation.

He also liked the ongoing, stimulating recollection of their night together.

And hoped it wouldn't be the last time, now that they were in each other's lives again.

But they weren't exactly together, and it would be better for Harper not to be in town for now, and maybe for a while.

Bryson made himself thrust aside that unwelcome but truthful thought as he finished getting things together to leave his condo for the day, including returning to his bedroom and sticking his wallet and phone into his pocket.

When he left the room, he didn't see Harper right

away. He wasn't surprised to find her in the guest bedroom, getting her things situated in her small suitcase and backpacks, including Lorrie's supplies, which she'd retrieved from the kitchen.

Oh, yes, she was preparing for what she anticipated would happen that day…and he did too, for her sake.

If all went well, she would stay at the shelter they were about to visit.

"Ready to go?" he asked her.

"Yes." She threw a smile toward him that didn't exactly look happy, but he figured he knew at least some of what she was thinking.

She was ready for this next stage in her life, if it hopefully came true.

And he would do what he could to ensure it did, and also attempt to get the questions causing her need to go there figured out.

"Then let's do it," he said. He bent to give Lorrie a brief pat between her ears, noting she already had a leash attached to a harness.

And then Bryson began helping Harper pick up her belongings and head toward the condo door.

Chapter 11

"I'm calling Kara now," Bryson said when they reached the still-closed condo door. Kneeling on the floor to pet Lorrie, Harper eavesdropped as Bryson told the assistant police chief that they were about to drive to the Chance Animal Shelter. "Good," he said in response to whatever Kara replied. "Thanks. I'll keep an eye out for them."

Harper assumed he meant the police patrols on the way. She attempted to keep herself calm while she thought about why they'd be out there—for her additional protection—but as she focused again on those threats, her blood pressure rose.

And she didn't calm down as Bryson next called Scott to also let him know they would be there soon.

Okay. Was the end of the car ride going to be the solution to her current problems?

Or would she be rejected from the shelter, as she feared? After all, she had already met Scott Sherridan, and he hadn't accepted her then. Why would he now?

Although…well, a little time had passed. Bryson had gotten to know her situation better, seen the threat that had most recently come in. Possibly told Scott about it.

And Scott had indicated a willingness to at least talk to her at the shelter.

"Okay," Bryson finally said. "Let's go."

Bryson picked up the dog bed, Harper's suitcase and one of her backpacks, after she had lifted the rest and grabbed Lorrie's leash. He did his usual thing of preceding her outside, then down the hallway toward the elevator, most likely listening for any odd sounds. No one else was in the hall, nor was anyone on the elevator when the two of them and the pup got on. Then down to the entry area, Bryson again ahead of them, and finally heading out the door cautiously and winding up in the parking lot, putting the items they carried into the rear of Harper's SUV and then getting inside themselves after Harper attached Lorrie's leash carefully to a seat belt in the back seat.

Was it wise to bring her belongings now? Harper certainly hoped so.

Bryson did the driving again. Harper wondered how he would get to Barky Boulevard later if Scott actually did accept her at the shelter. She'd let him borrow her car if needed.

For now, he drove at a moderate speed on the local Chance streets, even driving by Barky Boulevard.

"Everything looks okay there, right?" Harper asked, while wondering if it was in her best interests not to head directly to the shelter.

"Yes, it does," Bryson responded. "And I probably didn't have to check. Aunt Andrea would call me if anything seems wrong. But I'm also keeping my eyes open to see who's out on the roads here." He aimed a brisk nod in the direction of the doggy day care location, and Harper saw a police cruiser stopped on the opposite side of the street. She'd also noticed another cruiser go by after they left Bryson's condo.

She was definitely being protected by the local cops. She felt somewhat good about it, but still wished with all her heart that it wasn't necessary.

Well, they'd soon be at the shelter. They were on the move again, and she had learned enough about downtown Chance to know they were headed in that direction.

They soon reached the other side of the park from the shelter. And when they turned the corner of the narrow street, Bryson parked her car in the nearly empty lot in the shadows behind the shelter and pulled out his phone, then sent a text.

Harper was curious but didn't ask anything. After a return text sounded, he exited the car and so did she, and then got Lorrie out, noting that Bryson didn't remove her belongings yet. It made sense, until she learned if she had been accepted here.

Bryson let Lorrie sniff the pavement for a few seconds, then gestured for Harper to join him as he headed not toward what appeared to be the main entrance, a large gate at the far side of the parking lot, but to a smaller door at the other end of the lot. She wasn't surprised that he was able to open it right away, though she assumed, in a place like this, that all access points were kept locked most of the time. But that had probably been the goal of his text message, to let Scott know they had arrived.

They were soon inside the fence, and Bryson firmly shut the door behind them as someone stood there. It was an attractive lady in jeans and a navy blue Chance Animal Shelter T-shirt who had most likely unlocked the door. She had long brown hair pulled back behind her head and held by a thick blue hair tie. "Hi, Bryson. And I assume you are Harper, and Lorrie." As so many others did, the woman kneeled to pat Lorrie before continuing with any conversation.

"Yes, that's us," Harper said with a smile, figuring this woman greeting them must have some authority at the shelter.

"Harper, this is Nella Bresdall," Bryson said. "She works directly with Scott here at the shelter. She's sort of second in command."

Nella laughed. "Yes, you can kind of say that. But don't tell my buddy Scott."

"As if your guy doesn't know," Bryson countered.

Her guy. Harper figured there must be more between Scott and Nella than just first and second in command, or being buddies.

Which also meant it would be good for her to get to know Nella better and hopefully find a way to impress her with her integrity, and with her need for a safe place to stay for a while.

"Well, *my guy*—" Nella sang the words slightly, not denying them but attempting to make them sound funny. "He's waiting for us in his office. Mostly for you, Harper."

Harper figured that might be the case, and maybe a good thing…unless Scott was just following through with his conversations with Bryson without really intending to give her a chance here.

But Harper, as she began following Nella and Bryson, with Lorrie leashed beside her, hoped that *here* was the operative word.

Scott could have just insisted on talking with her

again at Barky Boulevard or somewhere else if he didn't intend to really give her a chance.

The path they were on just past the gate led between two fairly plain-looking concrete buildings, similar in appearance, each three or four stories high with windows facing the area. They seemed to be walking at the rear of the buildings, heading for the front, and the path soon opened onto a large, flat area containing additional paved pathways with chain-link fences and much shorter buildings on either side.

Harper saw maybe a half-dozen people out there, each walking dogs, but they remained too far away for her to get a good look at them. She let Lorrie do some sniffing, though she didn't allow the pup to delay them. She had to do everything needed to appear ready to follow instructions around here.

Nella and Bryson turned to the right, and they entered the building there, with Harper and Lorrie still following.

They wound up in a lobby that had some rooms off it, plus an elevator at the far side and a stairway leading upward. It seemed as plain as the outer areas, but Harper figured having a decorative place inside the shelter was not as important as making sure that whatever happened here was appropriate—for the people here as well as the animals.

Nella turned to Harper. "Are you okay with walking up the steps?"

Did she look physically injured, or was Nella just being kind? She hoped it was the latter.

Her only injuries at the moment were mental.

"Absolutely," she said brightly. "Lorrie too." Although she would help her pup if needed.

They were soon walking up the stairs, again behind Nella and Bryson. No problem, and they kept going to the top floor, the fourth. There, they walked past the first door, which Nella said contained the greeting office, as well as a few more that she said belonged to some managers.

When they reached the last one, at the end, she knocked on the wooden door.

It opened quickly, and Scott stood there. He made a gesture inviting them inside. "Come on in."

At least he appeared welcoming. Did he mean it?

Today, he wore jeans with a denim work shirt with a red-and-brown Chance Animal Shelter logo on its pocket, and the logo had the outline of a dog on it.

"Go ahead and sit down," he said. Surprisingly, the director's office wasn't very big and didn't have much furniture. It contained a metal desk that had an office chair behind it, and a computer and other equipment on top, plus several other chairs facing it.

Harper figured that the guests here, including her, were to sit facing the desk, and that was confirmed when Nella and Bryson headed that way.

Always a gentleman, Bryson pulled one of the chairs farther from the desk to make it easier for her to sit down, and Lorrie remained beside her on what appeared to be a laminated wood floor.

After they were seated, Bryson beside her, Nella on his other side, and Scott behind the desk, Harper wondered if she should start the conversation. She could thank Scott for letting her come today and start telling him more about what was going on with her.

But she felt relieved when Bryson was the one to begin. "Thanks for letting us come today, Scott."

Us? Well, he had brought her here, but she had the sense he visited the shelter fairly often. But maybe he was on some kind of schedule, and he hadn't planned on coming here today.

"Sure," Scott responded, looking at Harper and not Bryson. "I gather from speaking with Bryson that since we talked yesterday at Barky Boulevard you've received some further threats."

"That's right," Harper replied, attempting to remain calm. Or maybe she shouldn't. If her nervousness was more apparent, maybe Scott would be more likely to let her stay here. But in any case, she wanted to show those threats to Scott, so she started to pull her phone from her pocket.

"I assume you're going to open that nasty email so Scott and Nella can see it," Bryson said.

"That's right." This time Harper heard her own voice grow raspy and didn't attempt to change that. "As we discussed before," she continued, "sometimes the threats against me are sent in emails to my primary editors. I was in touch with them when I started checking my emails and apparently this time no one else has received anything. That's potentially a good thing for my career, but I can't be sure of it. And if I can't determine who's sending them, I can only assume I'm in some kind of danger without knowing what or from whom. And—"

"And we have no idea whether whoever it is has a sense of where Harper is right now," Bryson added. "We can only assume the worst until we figure out otherwise. As you know, the Chance PD is aware of the situation, and—"

"Yes, I've been in touch with Sherm and Kara," Scott said, "and they've expressed concern. I guess they're spending time and money trying to ensure no one is here in town ready to do something to harm Harper or anyone else."

"Which I really appreciate," Harper said.

"And my intent," Bryson said, "is to begin working with their online unit as soon as they'll let me, so we can hopefully track down the source."

Really? As helpful as Bryson had been, this was the first time Harper had heard this. And with his cop background, surely the local department would allow his participation that way.

"Good idea," Scott said. "Now, let's see that most recent threat."

Bryson watched as Harper stared at her phone and fiddled with it, evidently scrolling to find the most current email.

He wished he could do it for her so she didn't need to look at it again. Still, maybe her reading it once more, this time in Scott's presence, might be a good thing and help lead to her acceptance here at the shelter.

"I got quite a few before, like the one I already showed you, but I just received this one yesterday," she said quickly. She remained focused on the gadget in her hand, but her expression suggested she was scared.

She stood and held the phone out over the desk so

Scott could take it from her. He pulled it close so he could read it.

"So you're being told to stop writing, that some is good and some not, but you've been writing too much and for the wrong publications," Scott said. "And the last part, that whoever it is knows where you are and how to stop you for good... First of all, do you know who sent this?"

Bryson wanted to step in and tell Scott that if they did, Bryson would be out there finding that person and making sure he or she was taken into custody by the appropriate authorities.

But he knew Harper had to be in charge here, and do her own job of convincing Scott, and Nella too, that the threat was real, and from an unknown source. And also unknown was whether that person was lying about knowing where Harper was and how to stop her.

"No," Harper said, "I wish I did." She clasped her hands together on her lap, still holding Lorrie's leash. Though her voice was calm, her knuckles were white.

Bryson had an urge to reach over and hold one of those hands but remained still, watching her.

Nella watched her too and appeared caring and sympathetic. Bryson knew that Scott and she were an item. Maybe she could help convince him to let Harper stay.

"And if you did know who it was?" Scott prompted.

She scowled slightly as she continued. "I'd do whatever was necessary to stop them and make sure they did nothing to harm me or anyone else. Fortunately, the authorities, including Bryson, have been quite helpful recently as far as making sure no one is obviously after me here, but I can't be sure whoever it is won't find out

I'm in Chance if they don't know it yet. And I'm doing
my part by contacting those I know at the publications
who've received threats about me to try to figure out who
it is so I can make sure they're somehow stopped without hurting me. I recognize it's just scary communications so far, but I am actually scared there'll eventually
be more. And as much as I appreciate all that Bryson
has been doing, and the cops at the Chance PD, I'd just
like to settle down somewhere for a while until whoever
it is finally stopped or just gives up since they can't find
me. Like here, at the Chance Animal Shelter."

Bryson was impressed when Harper looked first at
Nella, with a slight, hopeful glance, and then stared Scott
straight in the eyes, as if daring him to say no, although
that might not have been the best way to get the response
she wanted.

"And you're not just sending yourself and your publishers ongoing threats with no physical follow-up to
get me to say yes and accept you to live here while you
research an article on what this shelter is really about?"
Scott's voice was chilly and even accusatory. He couldn't
really believe that. After all, Bryson had assured him
otherwise—and Scott had seemed to accept him as an
occasional volunteer here, a cop on leave who gave a
damn, so surely he'd believe him.

Maybe he just wanted Harper's reassurance before
accepting her.

"No," Harper said calmly, though Bryson believed
she wanted to burst out and criticize her doubter. "I've
told Bryson to let you know otherwise, and I'm sure
he did. I do want to continue writing if I stay here, but
I'll send things out remotely to my existing publishers

and do what research I can do online as well. Plus, I do have some stories already researched to some extent, and I can follow up with them." She paused, and again looked straight at Scott. "And it wouldn't hurt for me to do a story on the animal-shelter aspect of this place, as long as I didn't get into anything about the people here. I'd only go into how rescue animals are brought in and new homes are found for them. And if I did any story like that, I'd run it by you for your approval before submitting it anywhere."

Scott seemed to relax and even smiled a bit. "That's what I understood, but I wanted to hear it directly from you now. And while I wouldn't want to pry into your other stories or insist on access to your computer if I invite you to stay here…"

"You'd prefer making sure I didn't say one thing but do something else." Harper smiled back, and, though she didn't appear to relax much, Bryson had the sense she wasn't quite as tense as before. "Look, I couldn't and wouldn't give you access to all my emails and other communications online. That's too personal. But you've said you have read some of my articles, and I wouldn't mind letting an animal-shelter executive like you read and comment on new articles before I send them out, at least for now."

"I appreciate that," Scott said. "And I appreciate your issues and why you'd like to stay here for now." His head tilted as he continued. "Look. As I've said, I know it could all be a farce. Despite the emailed threats you've showed us, there've evidently been no indications of actual physical threats against you—"

"Which is a good thing," Bryson interrupted.

"Yes, if it's all real," Scott agreed, still looking at Harper. "I still hope you're not lying. And, well, over time, I think I've come to read people's emotions from their faces at least a bit, and I believe I've seen actual fear in your eyes." He stood then, glanced at Nella, who smiled at him, then held his hand out to her over his desk. "So, Harper, consider yourself a new staff member here at the Chance Animal Shelter."

"Really?" Harper was standing now too. Instead of reaching out to grab and shake Scott's hand, she maneuvered around Lorrie and hurried around the desk, where she gave him a brief hug.

Bryson had a big grin on his face, along with an urge to go hug both of them, and also Nella, who'd joined them. Instead, he stood and looked at Scott. "Thanks," he said. "And I'll continue to do my damnedest to figure out what's going on and remove the threats from Harper's life."

Chapter 12

Harper didn't even attempt to hide her relief and happiness at being accepted as a staff member at the Chance Animal Shelter.

Hugs? Sure. She wanted to do more by helping, if she could figure out what they needed.

For they were truly helping her.

Not that living here would solve all her problems, but at least she had some time to figure them out without feeling under immediate threat. Since she didn't know how close or knowledgeable her adversary was, worrying about it overwhelmed her at times. Now, at least she would have walls around her and people whose job was to protect staff members, including her.

And as much as she appreciated Bryson and his help, she hopefully wouldn't need to worry about his safety too.

"Let's take care of some details first."

Really? Like what? But Harper wasn't really surprised that new staff members had to sign an agreement, a copy of which Scott handed her.

Reading it, she also wasn't surprised it contained a commitment not to tell the world what this place was about. It applied to everyone who was being helped here, not just journalists.

Well, she'd already agreed to that, although if she ever decided it was time to write a story about the animal-shelter part of the place, she'd run it by Scott, as she'd promised.

For now, she finished reading the agreement, which wasn't very long.

She noticed that Scott had put a line through a part that said the staff member signing the agreement agreed not to have any contact with the outside world, by phone, computer, or otherwise. Harper looked at Scott. "I appreciate your eliminating the provisions that wouldn't allow me to continue writing and submitting stories."

"But look at what I added on the addendum at the back."

The extra printed page was short and simply referenced that Harper would limit use of her phone or emails to contacts necessary for her profession, and would be discreet in what she said in all calls, texts and other communications. And she was, and could remain, a journalist while here, but she would run all stories by shelter management before submitting them.

The language didn't limit this to stories about the shelter, but Harper understood.

Scott would want to make certain that she wasn't lying about what she was submitting. Which, of course, she wouldn't. And he would most likely also want to be kept aware of whom she was in contact with, and how.

She didn't really like being under keen observation, but understood it, as well as Scott's ability to tell her no and even stop her from using her means of outside contact, which were also addressed there.

Well, she'd known she'd be giving up aspects of privacy and more if she stayed here under protection. She'd just have to live with it.

For now.

Another part of the agreement explained she'd be given a new identity, and before she could ask about that, Scott apparently realized where she was in her reading.

"Before you sign the document, we'll go ahead and figure out who you'll be while you're here."

Harper laughed. "I hope I can just be me."

"Yep, but you won't be Harper Morsley. And I understand they call you Hanna at Barky Boulevard, and that won't work either. But I've some ideas for a new name for you."

Really? Harper wondered what they were, and how she would feel to now have essentially three names. Well, she'd been a writer for a long time, and many writers took pseudonyms, though for different reasons than this.

"Hey, how about if we call her Lorrie?" Bryson inserted. As the dog looked up from the floor, where she'd been sleeping, Harper laughed along with the others.

"Oh, I think we should decide on something else so my poor pup doesn't get even more confused than she is," Harper said.

"I agree," Nella said, moving so she could be the next to give Lorrie a brief pat. "I also came up with a few ideas, although if you have any, feel free to run them by us."

Clearly, Nella was very involved with running the

place, and Harper appreciated that. But would she appreciate any name Nella suggested for her?

"How do you like Isabella, or Connie, or Phyllis?" Nella asked, and Scott also mentioned a couple. Harper found herself glancing toward Bryson in case he glommed on to any of them. The ones she heard at first seemed okay though not ideal. Bryson mostly watched the exchange and scowled, apparently not thrilled with this aspect of what they were doing.

But as they continued, Harper found herself zeroing in on a name that didn't sound at all like her real one, though she liked it well enough to possibly use someday as a pseudonym in her writing once this was over with.

Assuming it ever was over with.

She wound up combining a suggested first name and last name. "How about if I become Mia Myerson?"

She glanced immediately at Bryson to see his reaction. He was smiling, a good thing.

And the others' reactions?

"Sounds fine with me," Scott said.

"I like it," said Nella.

"So now I have to stop thinking of you as Harper or Hanna," Bryson added, his grin even wider.

"Yes, you will, or at least that's what you'll need to call me around here." Harper—Mia?—figured she would only see Bryson, and those here at the shelter, for a while.

Or would she see Bryson here? He wasn't a manager or a staff member, although she'd already figured he helped out here some both with his cop background and appreciation of animal rescue.

But would he have any reason to come here for a while?

To see her? Ha!

Well, in any event, Harper thought, she would soon become Mia to Scott and Nella and everyone she met here at the shelter, and to Bryson.

Since they were done discussing the agreement and Mia's new identity, Scott had her sign two copies, using both names.

"Now," he said when she finished, "I'll keep one of these for you, but right now I'll turn you over to Nella to introduce you to our facilities, plus maybe some of the people and animals we shelter here."

"Absolutely," Nella said.

"That sounds great." Harper/Mia didn't want to gush too much but figured it wouldn't hurt to continue to show gratitude.

All of them but Scott headed toward the door.

"I'll show you around now, then take you to your new apartment," Nella said as they left Scott's office.

She already had an apartment assigned? That was wonderful. It wouldn't feel as good as staying in Bryson's condo, especially considering the special perks she had engaged in with him, but it hopefully would be private and quiet and good for Lorrie too. And safe.

"Okay if I join you on your tour?" Bryson asked as the four of them, including Lorrie, walked past the other, still empty, offices on the fourth floor. Harper wondered who used them, and when.

"Of course." Nella smiled at him. "I assumed you would. You know your way around here, so you can help me make sure Mia knows what's where when we're finished, or at least the important stuff."

"Like where she can get her food."

Harper enjoyed listening to their banter, so she didn't join in for the moment. With Lorrie, she preceded Nella into the elevator after the other woman's gesture in that direction. Bryson was the last to enter, and they were soon on their way to the bottom floor.

"As an introduction," Nella said, "we'll walk around the grounds first and I'll show you the various buildings where our animals are sheltered. I'm sure we'll run into some staff members, since their job is to help take care of those animals, so they often take dogs for walks. And after that, we'll come back to this front area and I'll take you to your apartment."

"Sounds wonderful," Harper said as they went outside, Lorrie sniffing the ground. "I assume you'll introduce me as Mia, so I need to start thinking of myself that way."

As a skilled journalist, she sometimes had to pretend her background was different in order to get people to relate to her and inform her about what she asked concerning animals and rescues and other relevant topics.

So... She was now Mia, and did need to start thinking of herself that way so as not to screw things up.

Mia scanned the location as well as she could, noted the long walkway down the center with small buildings on one side and people walking dogs along the pavement.

She was impressed when Nella pointed out the main reception building, where people hoping to adopt pets, and others planning to stay here, mostly were welcomed, and indicated they also had a small veterinary clinic there. It was near the office building, and not far away was the taller concrete building containing apartments. "We also have an eating area on the ground floor there," she told Harper...er, Mia. "Eating area for people, that is."

"Then I'll need to check it out," Mia said with a laugh.

"Of course, we have plenty of food for the animals under our protection too. And we can make certain you have enough for Lorrie in your apartment." She smiled down at the pup, which made Mia smile too.

"Do many staff members keep their own pets?" Mia had wondered about that. She knew she was already being treated differently from most people under protection here. Was this another aspect of it?

It was. "No, although we encourage our staff members to spend a lot of time with the sheltered pets to help get them acclimated for potential adoptions outside here, and most wind up having favorites. But it's rare to have our staffers bring their own pets."

They now walked along the path in the middle of the enclosed shelter, and Mia made sure that Lorrie, on her leash, stayed right beside her. When they reached the first concrete building on the left, a couple of people stood off to the side of the door. They were apparently working on training a dog, since one of them, an older lady wearing jeans and a blue Chance Animal Shelter T-shirt, had her hand raised as if holding a treat, and the small gray poodle mix in front of her sat looking up at her hand, but wasn't moving. The other woman, younger and rather pretty and also wearing a Chance Animal Shelter T-shirt, a yellow one, was also praising the dog, whose name was Ashy.

"Let's watch for a minute," Nella said.

Mia was glad when Bryson stood beside her on the sidewalk, also observing the training, and at Mia's instruction Lorrie sat and watched too.

"That's something else we have our staff members

do," Nella said softly. "In addition to walking dogs and feeding all the animals and otherwise taking care of them, we train them to train the dogs."

The dog they called Ashy stood on command, then sat again, then lied down. After a few minutes, Nella said, "Let's go introduce you to them."

"Great," Mia said. She figured she would be hanging out with these women and others at the shelter for a while, and she was eager to meet them, and make notes in her head, although she wouldn't be writing about what she saw. Or at least, if she did, she wouldn't identify the location as here.

They approached the woman and dog. "Hey," Nella said, "I want to introduce you to a new staff member."

"And dog? Another shelter pup?" asked the older woman.

"Kind of," Nella said, "but the circumstances are such that our new staffer had to bring her dog for their safety. The dog is Lorrie, and our new staff member is Mia. Mia, this is Kathy." She gestured toward the older woman who had just spoken. "And that is Chessie."

Chessie, the pretty, younger woman, responded first. "Welcome, Mia. I'd love to know what brought you here, but we're not allowed to ask or talk about it. But just be sure you'll be well taken care of here, as we all are. And we're all good friends."

"Absolutely," Kathy said. "Yes, welcome."

Bryson observed Harper's—no, Mia's—interaction with these couple of staff members and the dog they were working with. He'd met Kathy and Chessie before and knew they were genuine staff members under protection. In fact, he had talked with Scott now and then on his visits about those under protection, and he believed that Chessie was here thanks to her abusive ex-husband. Bryson hadn't heard why Kathy, the thin older lady, was there, but figured there was a good reason, as with everyone else.

He wasn't surprised when Kathy and Chessie also fussed over Lorrie in a cute way. From what he had seen, they, and probably everyone under protection at the animal and human shelter, liked animals as well as the other people being cared for here, so why not like a new dog as well?

They didn't hang out there long though. Nella continued their stroll down the paved walkway, pointing out the other buildings for animals and letting Mia go inside briefly to glimpse the medium-sized and larger dogs, as well as the cats and other animals being cared for in the farthest structure.

"Okay, then, Mia," Nella finally said. "Let's go back so you can see the most important places here, especially for a newcomer—the cafeteria, and then your new apartment."

"Sounds great," Mia/Harper said. Okay, Bryson would force himself to start thinking of her as Mia so he wouldn't make any mistakes around anyone else, but just like he hadn't started thinking of her as Hanna at Barky Boulevard despite her being introduced there that way, she would always be Harper to him.

They headed back down the path they'd just walked along, toward the administration building area. On the way, a few other staff members passed, walking dogs. Bryson wasn't surprised that Nella introduced Mia to them. He had met most of them too, though he didn't know them well. But it was a good thing for Mia to get to know them and hopefully become friends.

It didn't take long to reach their destination. Nella led them into the apartment building with the cafeteria downstairs and showed it to Mia. It was midafternoon, so no one was seated at any of the long parallel tables in the middle of the dining room, nor did he think there was anything on the side table along the wall that at mealtime held food that could be picked up by those dining there. Another table near it held drinks including water, and that, at least, seemed to be filled, presumably in case anyone out caring for the animals got thirsty and popped in, although he would be surprised if any coffee there was hot.

"Looks inviting," Mia said.

"Definitely. I'll meet you at dinnertime and accompany you in to show you around better and meet more people."

"Thanks." And Mia did sound grateful. Bryson assumed she was for everything around here that she'd been shown and otherwise. And he understood that.

Even though he'd have done his damnedest to keep her safe, she was undoubtedly a lot safer here than in his care.

"Okay, next stop," Nella said. "Let's go to your new apartment."

Though Bryson had popped in at the shelter fairly often, and recently, mostly just to familiarize himself with it and assure Scott that, cop that he still was, kind of, he would do everything possible to make sure the facility and its residents remained safe, he had only seen the outside of the apartment building and not any of the units.

Now, he would get to see an apartment. And vowed not to let himself feel bad that the woman he used to care for, who was back in his life, and with whom he had made love, was going to move in there and be away from him again.

After all, he wouldn't be that far from this shelter. And he would continue to visit here to help with its security, and now that would include Harper, er, Mia too.

Nella led them out of the cafeteria and into the entry hallway to the apartment building. "Your place is on the third floor," she said.

"Sounds good," Mia said, and she followed Nella, holding Lorrie's leash, to the stairway, making sure her pup had no trouble.

Bryson followed them, glancing down the hallways to the other apartments. No one was out there now. He wondered how many were occupied.

The apartment Nella led them to was the second door on the right, and she opened it with a key card, which she handed to Mia. Bryson continued to follow them, this time inside the unit.

It appeared pleasant enough, furnished with a nice but not particularly stylish gray sofa and couple of chairs, a small coffee table and a TV mounted on the wall, with a laminated wooden floor below. He also followed as Nella showed Mia around, pointing out the kitchen, with its tile floor and counter, metal sink and refrigerator, and even a microwave oven. She opened the doors to a couple of the wooden cabinets and pointed out some plastic dishes, then opened some drawers to show flatware and utensils, such as a can opener.

"Looks like everything we'll need," Mia said. "I've got Lorrie's bowls and food, and—"

"And as for your food, you can pick up some stuff at the cafeteria for times you would rather eat here."

"Great." Mia did look pleased.

Nella next took them down the short hall to point out a couple small bedrooms and the bathroom that had a tub and shower, complete with a curtain as well as towels hung on the rods. "There's some soap in the cabinet there," she told Mia. "Hopefully, you already have any cosmetics you'll want."

"Definitely."

Back in the main bedroom, Nella reached into the closet and pulled out two Chance Animal Shelter T-shirts. "Here's what you'll wear while you're here."

Mia ducked into the bathroom and exchanged the shirt she had been wearing for a blue shelter shirt.

And then they were done, except that Bryson said, "I'll go out to Mia's car and bring in the few things she brought."

"I'll join you," Nella said.

"Me too," added Mia, and before Nella could object, she said, "That way I can also take Lorrie for another walk…and you can tell me a little more about the schedule around here, like when I can join in working with some of the animals. Hopefully, Lorrie can come along too."

"Of course."

All that took maybe another twenty minutes. They got all of Mia's things to her new apartment, and first she removed Lorrie's bowls and food from one of the backpacks. Bryson had carried the dog's bed upstairs, so it looked like Lorrie, at least, was all set.

But then... Well, he knew he had spent a lot of time helping Mia move here. He had to get back to Barky Boulevard that afternoon.

He wished he could stay longer, maybe even for dinner in that cafeteria. But he knew that wasn't a good idea, at least not for now.

"So let me know if there's anything you need that you don't see here," Nella told Mia as they stood in the kitchen as Lorrie lapped some water from her bowl.

"I will. Thank you so much. And we'll come back downstairs in a little while, after I unpack a bit, so I can learn more about how things around here work."

"Sounds good," Nella said. "See you soon." She started to leave, then said goodbye to Bryson before walking out the apartment door.

And then, Bryson was alone with the woman he had slept with last night. Who knew when he would even see her again, let alone dare to hope that they'd—

Never mind about that.

"I'd better get going too," he told her, then found himself looking deeply into her gorgeous green eyes as she drew close to him.

"Will I— I mean, I know I'll be staying here for now, maybe for a long time. Do you visit here much?"

"Sometimes," he said, and figured it would be a lot more now.

"Good. I'll look forward to seeing you whenever. And thanks so much for all you've already done."

"I'm not through with it," he said, staring firmly down

at her. "I understand you'll have phone and email access. I want you to keep in touch with me both ways, and forward any questionable communications to me so I can check out their sources as best I can. And—"

Mia had grabbed him behind his neck and pulled him down so they were suddenly engaged in a very heated kiss. He loved the feel of her warm lips searching his, her tongue, her curved body against him.

And after a time that wasn't long enough, when she pulled away, he decided he would be back soon.

Very soon.

Chapter 13

He's gone, Mia thought a short while later as she started putting some things into the bedroom closet and dresser drawers while Nella, who had returned almost immediately, saying she'd changed her mind about leaving and had decided to show Mia around now, played with Lorrie.

That was probably a good thing. He would be safer that way, no longer in her company, so she wouldn't need to worry that he would take her place in her enemy's crosshairs if that enemy did indeed have a sense of where Harper was.

Harper, not Mia.

And regarding Bryson? Well, they'd kind of indicated they would stay in touch, plus he said he wanted her to forward any more threats she received so he could continue to try to find the source, and deal with it.

She appreciated that. She appreciated *him*.

And missed him already, and didn't know when, if ever, they would see each other in person again.

Safer for him. Sadder for her.

Okay, she needed to get her mind off Bryson, and back on her life as it would be for now.

Mia was glad that Nella was with her, and that she

continued to play with Lorrie, giving her frequent commands like "Sit," "Down," and "Come here and hug me." Meanwhile, Mia finished putting enough stuff away that she felt comfortable about starting her new life at the shelter…sort of. And though she wanted to go back downstairs and act like a staff member, and learn more of what that was about, she also wanted to return to this apartment before dinner and be Harper online for a while as well.

"Okay," she finally said to Nella, "I'm through here. Could we go back downstairs? I'd love to learn more about the shelter and its inhabitants, and do my own playing with the dogs and learn how they're trained here."

"That's why I came back." Nella rose from where she'd been kneeling on the floor beside Lorrie. "I think it's a good thing for you to learn about this place, only…"

"Only you'd like more reassurance I'll keep what I learn to myself and not stick it all into an article without running it by Scott, right?" She saw Nella's pretty but concerned brown eyes look down as if she was embarrassed, which was sweet but unnecessary. "I get it. But I've promised Scott, and now I'll promise you too, that I won't do anything to throw information about this wonderful place out there in a way that might harm it, and yes, if I ever do write an article about this animal shelter, I'll get Scott's okay to make sure I don't inadvertently include anything I shouldn't."

"I figured. And though I always worry about everything and everyone around here, animals included, I don't really doubt your intentions."

Didn't she? Well, no matter. Harper knew she was serious, and she remained Harper as a journalist. Mia would do all she could to make sure things around here went well too, for herself and anyone she could help, both animals and people.

"What would you suggest I do for the rest of the afternoon, till dinner?" she asked Nella as they headed toward the door. Mia was amused that Nella was the one who took Lorrie's leash off the coffee table in the living room and slipped it on her.

Obviously, the woman cared about Lorrie. Being one of the managers here, she probably cared a lot for most dogs, and other pets too.

And the staff members as well, Mia figured.

"I think it would make sense for you to work with some of the others here as they train dogs. That way, you can get to know both people and dogs better, as well as what we're up to here. That's what we generally have new staff members start with, unless they clearly prefer cats or some of the smaller pets being cared for. And considering you're Lorrie's mom, I think I can assume you're more of a dog person."

"You got it," Mia said. And she would do just as Nella said, for a while. But she would either get tired, or need a potty break, or something soon, before dinner, so she could spend a little while on her computer.

It felt strange and a little sad to leave her apartment and go downstairs and walk around the facility without Bryson alongside her, but she had to get used to it.

Being here, without his direct protection, or presence, was her life now, and maybe for a long time.

Unless, somehow, she could figure out the source of her issues as fast as she wanted.

Probably a pipe dream, and she realized it. But she would do her damnedest to make it come true.

Mia saw a bunch of people at the far side of the walkway, each leading a dog. "Let's go see who's there," Nella said, "and I'll introduce you to some of those you haven't met."

Exactly what Mia anticipated. She was glad, and not surprised, that the people included Kathy, with Ashy the poodle mix, and Chessie with a Labrador retriever mix named Moe. Also there was Leonard, a rather young man with longish brown hair who had a Jack Russell terrier mix with him named Russell.

And yes, this was a doggy training session. Mia figured that someday she would need to bring out one of the dogs cared for by the shelter and work with him, help to teach him commands to make sure he behaved…and could be adopted as soon as possible. She'd figure out where to leave Lorrie then, maybe just in their apartment, or maybe with one of the other staff members.

Other staff members. Yes, she was now a staff member. She was no longer just an out-there journalist. In fact, she hopefully would remain a journalist, but her out-there part would be all on the computer screen, not in actuality.

Computer screen. Not that she needed a reminder, but she was eager to return to her apartment and engage in that part of her life as well.

But for now… She turned to Nella. "Should I just watch for now to see how these experienced trainers do their thing? I hope to learn enough to start working with some of the dogs here, maybe tomorrow, if that's okay."

"Sounds okay to me, although I think giving it a try now would be better."

Still, Mia just stood at first and observed as the staffers each worked with their current canine students. Nothing appeared out of the ordinary, and Mia had, in addition to training Lorrie, worked with other dogs and observed similar sessions when researching articles.

She believed she would do just fine when she took over some training at a different time.

And after a while, she felt ready to thank everyone and return inside, but instead Nella took Lorrie's leash. "Why don't you just give it a try now?"

Mia felt uncomfortable saying no, and so, at Nella's suggestion, she began working with Russell.

Oh, yes, the terrier was as energetic as Jack Russells tended to be, so it took all of Mia's concentration and energy to work with the pup, but she enjoyed it. A lot. Despite the fact she wanted to head to her apartment.

And she did it for a while, as the others there also continued training the dogs in their charge.

She also heard that they'd had another Jack Russell mix at the shelter who'd been named Jack, and who had recently been adopted, making all his human friends glad. Adoptions here sounded frequent, enabling them to bring in more rescues. People stayed longer though.

When their training started winding down, Nella asked Mia to join them as they took Russell back to his enclosure, so she could also see how that went.

Okay, another delay.

There were other dogs in the sizable enclosure in the building where smaller dogs were housed, and Kathy brought Ashy there as well, with Nella remaining in charge of Lorrie, and Mia with Russell.

And when they'd secured the dogs inside their fencing, Nella told Mia it was time to grab dinner.

Which made her sigh. She could stand to eat, but that was yet another delay in her getting onto the computer.

Oh, well. Mia recognized that, while she was here, she had to fit in with the other staff members and their schedules. Today was just the start.

She took Lorrie back from Nella, and since Nella didn't say otherwise, she assumed it was okay to bring her dog into the cafeteria.

She'd already seen what the place looked like, but when they returned inside now it was filled with people, most of whom she hadn't met yet, and all wearing Chance Animal Shelter T-shirts. Many were seated at the long parallel tables, while others stood with plates in their hands at the table along the wall where Mia understood the food would be available to dish out.

"For now, why don't you just plan on sitting with the people you've met… Kathy, Chessie and Leonard?" Nella told her. "I think they'll be sitting together. You'll meet others at your table too."

"Sounds good." Mia followed those three to the food, and was pleased to say hi to a few other people who greeted her as the newcomer she was. She hoped she'd remember a lot of their names but figured it might take a while.

Standing alongside some of the others also getting their meals, Mia put some meat loaf and mashed potatoes onto her plate, and small pieces of roast beef, which she would share with Lorrie, who fortunately didn't get very energetic leashed by her side despite having her nose in the air a lot—she was apparently enjoying the smell of the food above her.

"Oh, hey," Leonard soon said, turning to her. "I know you don't know everyone here, but I do want to make one introduction."

A middle-aged lady in, unsurprisingly, a red Chance Animal Shelter shirt but with a white apron over it, stood at the end of the table, and Leonard led Mia and Lorrie around others toward her.

"Hi," the woman said. "You're new here. I'm Sara, and I'm the primary cook, so if you have any thoughts or problems about the food, please let me know."

"Hi, Sara. I'm Mia." Mia was glad she didn't hesitate at all with her name. "And everything looks great. I'm sure I'll enjoy it."

"Your dog too, I hope," Sara said, smiling down at Lorrie. She apparently had no problem with the pup being near the food.

Soon, Mia sat near one end of the table with the most people, including those she'd hoped to hang out with, since she'd met them before: Kathy, Leonard and Chessie. All three welcomed her, but they also proceeded to converse with others about some dogs, including a few who'd been at the shelter for a while, and others who'd only recently been brought in to be cared for and rehomed.

Mia found the conversation interesting but had nothing to contribute. Her mind remained at work researching, though, as it did in similar situations, where she could learn about shelter animals and their environment and care.

For now, she had to stuff what she heard to the back of her mind. She would probably never be able to use it even though it was all interesting.

Her appetite was soon satisfied and she felt comfortable taking brief control of the discussion to let her buddies here know she was about to leave. "Got to take Lorrie for another walk, then get a bit more organized in my new apartment," she said as she stood and smiled from one person to the next.

And she, of course, didn't tell them what else she planned to do in her apartment.

"What do I do with my dishes?" she asked Chessie, who was beside her.

"I'll show you." Chessie also rose, taking her own plate.

"Oh, I didn't mean to disturb your eating," Mia said.

"You didn't. I'll show you, then get some more food for myself."

Leading both Mia and Lorrie, Chessie showed her into the large kitchen area that had lots of food-preparation gadgetry, plus an area off to the side with a large sink. "Scrape your remnants off there for compost," she said, "and put your dish into the sink." Mia did so.

They returned to the dining area, and Mia headed to Scott and Nella, who were sitting together with some other people, most of whom Mia didn't recognize. "Thanks so much for everything, including this delicious dinner," Mia told them.

"Are you heading to your apartment now?" Nella asked.

"Soon as Lorrie and I walk for a minute."

Nella and Scott smiled at her, their expressions caring and curious, but didn't mention what she figured they knew she would be doing: checking her computer.

"Guess we'll see you next for breakfast," Scott said. "Right here. And you can join us as early as eight a.m."

"Sounds good." And in, fact, it did, although Mia wanted to start planning her own schedule here as soon as she could.

It was only around six thirty, so she should be able to spend a significant amount of time on her computer before bedtime, including starting to write some of the articles she had been researching before coming here. For now, though, she walked Lorrie away from the cafeteria and down the pathway for a short distance, watching the area and listening for traffic outside the tall fence and also hearing a few dog barks.

Since it was June, plenty of light remained outside, but she didn't really see anything or anyone out there. Presumably, people here were at dinner or in their apartments.

Mia didn't spend a lot of time walking on the pathway but headed to the building she had just left without getting near the cafeteria area. Instead, she entered the apartment lobby and was soon upstairs with Lorrie. She made sure her apartment door was locked behind her, and then she sat on the sofa with her laptop on the coffee table.

She'd had her phone with her this whole time but kept it muted since most others here weren't allowed to keep phones on them. She checked it now. No missed calls or texts.

She turned on her computer and got into her emails. She recognized the sources of most, fortunately. Not too much spam, but were any of the ones she didn't know from whoever had been threatening her?

Well, she would find out soon.

But first, she saw several from Wanda Grey, the editor of *Pet Rescue Forever*, where Harper had received those bad reviews.

She liked that magazine. She liked Wanda. She wanted to keep her relationship there going and continue to submit new articles when she could.

And so she began opening those emails first.

And gasped.

Wanda was definitely angry with her. I've received more bad reviews of your article, she said in the first one. Some threats against me and Pet Rescue Forever. Where are you? I want you to come here immediately and work with me on getting things fixed. More articles. Better ones. Right away.

When Harper hadn't responded right away, that apparently made Wanda even angrier. You've really harmed my magazine, she said in her next communication. You need to come here and fix it or I'll come after you and fix you.

Harper had always been friendly with Wanda before, or so she thought.

But now she had a really bad feeling. Was Wanda the one who had been threatening her from the beginning?

Harper—yes, she was again thinking of herself as Harper—pulled her phone out. Like it or not, time to make a call.

Bryson was having dinner with his aunt at a casual restaurant not far from Barky Boulevard when his cell phone vibrated in his pocket. He mostly kept it on silent while at the doggy day care, so any calls wouldn't bother dogs he might be working with, assuming they even paid attention.

But Aunt Andrea would, and he didn't want to bother her either.

Now though, he lifted his phone from his pocket as he sat on his side of the booth and glanced at it.

Harper. Yes, he still had her real name on his phone and most likely wouldn't change it.

But why was she calling? Was she even allowed to, from the shelter?

He was well aware she was allowed to access her computer, so probably her phone too.

Maybe she just wanted to say hi.

Maybe not.

"I've got a call coming in," he told his aunt. "I'd better take it." He tried to sound serious—did sound serious—as if wanting to convey the call was important, maybe from his old employer, the LAPD.

And it was important.

"Is it Hanna?" Aunt Andrea was definitely smart. But it wouldn't be a good idea to let her know even part of the truth. "Hanna" had supposedly headed back to her home for a while.

Andrea didn't know she was at the shelter, or that she had a reason to be.

But Bryson didn't want to lie to her. "Yeah, we promised to keep in touch" was all he said. And rather than continue to sit there and let Andrea eavesdrop on a conversation that probably wouldn't just be a friendly hello, he said, "I'll be right back," without offering any further explanation.

Their dinner was already on the table, and they'd begun eating—hamburgers for both of them and beer to drink. That was good. Andrea would be able to keep busy.

Bryson stood and headed around the nearby tables to the restaurant's front door, ignoring the loud murmur of the crowd as he answered the phone.

"Hello?" He didn't mention a name, not knowing where Harper/Mia might be, and if anyone could be eavesdropping.

"Bryson?" Harper's tone was soft and hoarse, and he could tell immediately that something was wrong.

"Where are you?" he demanded, keeping his voice low so as not to attract any attention. "What's going on?"

"I'm sure you can guess," she choked out. "I helped to train a dog here and mingle with some of the staff members, then had dinner with the group, and finally got the opportunity to return to my apartment with Lorrie and sit down at the computer. And—"

"And you got some threatening emails." Bryson's shoulders stiffened, and he had an urge to go there and take her into his arms and protect her.

"Yes, but it wasn't what I expected. And I haven't even looked at all the emails I received."

"Tell me what you're talking about," he insisted, wanting to hop into his car and get to the shelter right away.

But it wasn't what he expected either. Oh, he was aware of those nasty reviews she had been receiving, but the editor at that magazine had been more upset than angry, from what he'd understood.

Before.

Maybe. Could she be the one who'd been threatening Harper from the start?

"Forward what she said to me," he demanded. "And any other questionable emails you may have received, once you check them all out. I've got some ideas what to do about them."

Did he really? Well, he'd been pondering the situation for a while now. But he had to admit to himself that so far, he had no answers.

But he would develop them even faster now.

He had to.

He had already taken on protecting Harper, and having her become a staff member at the Chance Animal Shelter might not be enough.

Well, Bryson would stay involved. Get more involved.

And make certain, no matter where she was, that Harper stayed safe.

Chapter 14

Forward those emails to Bryson?

What could he do about them?

Read them, sure, and see the ire that Wanda was now subjecting Harper to.

Not that she wanted to see the most recent critical reviews or threats. And Harper hadn't even looked at her other emails to see if they contained anything worse.

Still… Well, she had been the one to call Bryson, out of panic.

Now, she had to deal with it.

While she continued to deal in her mind with her crumbling career. Wanda was the second of her three primary editors who now hated her, or at least wanted things to change in their current professional relationship.

But what could Harper—

"Harper? Are you okay?" Bryson sounded highly concerned, and it was no wonder. Harper had called him, mentioned her latest problem, and was now dwelling on it internally without really communicating with the kind, caring man who had started to help her-and more.

"I—I'm sorry, Bryson," she said. "I should probably make notes on what I'm feeling now. Maybe I could use the description somehow in an article when I'm writing about a particularly difficult situation with animals I'm researching." She attempted to sound amusing, and not as highly stressed as she actually felt.

It didn't work.

"Stop trying to be funny and tell me what's going on," he pleaded. "Do those emails indicate you're in danger right now? I can head to the shelter and be there in around twenty minutes, maybe less. And—"

"I'm not in danger," Harper said, and hoped it was true. "Although my career seems to keep getting more endangered. I'm just… Well, I probably shouldn't have called you, but I needed a friendly ear to hear my concerns."

"My ear is definitely friendly," Bryson responded. "The rest of me too. Look, I really want to help you. Go ahead and forward those emails to me, and I'll take a look and give you a call back so we can discuss what should come next."

Harper didn't even attempt to let Bryson know the extent of her appreciation for his being there for her, even though he wasn't right there. But he wanted to help her. As usual.

"Okay," she said, trying to sound as normal as possible. "That makes sense. Is this a good time for you to go over them?"

"Sure. It's late enough in the day that we've pretty much shut down Barky Boulevard. I may take a little while to get back to you since we're out having dinner. And it makes more sense for me to be at my condo so I can concentrate on what you send and discuss it with you. But if you need for me to do it right away, I can tell Andrea that—"

"No, just do what you need to enjoy your dinner and

help your aunt finish for the day. I'm okay with your doing what you have to and then getting back to me." She hoped, but she wouldn't mention any doubts to him. Instead she added, "Now you go ahead, and I'll send the stuff soon."

Probably after she'd gone over the other emails to see if they contained anything else bad. If so, she'd send them too.

"If you're sure—"

"I'm sure. Talk to you later." She looked forward to it, especially since she would have to reread the emails from Wanda, which were bad enough to make her feel needy. At least in need of Bryson's calming voice.

Too bad she couldn't have his calming presence too, though it had been kind of him to offer.

And if there were more bad emails…

Well, it was time to find out.

She had a good excuse for delaying though. It was always time to take Lorrie outside, unless she'd just been out a few minutes before. It had been nearly an hour now, and if it was actually less, Harper could lie about something as petty as that to herself.

And so, glad they were here at the safe and secure Chance Animal Shelter, Harper called to her pup. "Out, Lorrie?"

As anticipated, Lorrie seemed excited about the idea, as she often was, wagging her small butt of a tail as Harper got her harness and leash and fastened them on her.

There was no one in the hallway, and Harper made sure the door was locked behind them. No, Mia did. Outside her apartment here, she had to continuously think of herself as Mia.

She led Lorrie down the steps from the third floor, not wanting to get into the elevator despite the downstairs climb not being easy for her short-legged girl, and they were soon outside.

And alone there too. No one was walking other dogs or hanging around near the cafeteria, apartments or nearby buildings.

No interruptions then, which was a good thing. Mia knew she had to get back and read those emails and forward the ones she'd already received, and any others that were problems, to Bryson.

And suck in her emotions, not let her fears interfere with getting the help she needed.

As usual, Lorrie was a good girl, and though she did sniff around a few minutes, she took care of business and then seemed fine with getting back inside.

And then, Mia had no further excuses for not getting onto her computer.

No. Once more, she was Harper. In fact, since she hadn't seen anyone on this venture outside, she'd probably remained Harper since her last check of her computer, and her conversation with Bryson.

She got herself a glass of water from the sink, adding ice from the freezer. Okay, yet another delay, but this one didn't last long. And the taste of water, wetting her otherwise dry mouth, felt good.

She sat down on the sofa, put the computer on her lap and opened it, then turned it on. The Wi-Fi worked fine, since she was able to access her emails immediately.

And she took a deep breath.

First thing, she took another look at the emails from Wanda. Harper recognized that Wanda got angrier when she didn't hear back from her right away.

Like Macie Smithston did when Harper didn't immediately drop everything and run to her editorial office to help deal with the threatening emails received by *Puppies, Kittens and Humans*.

Harper understood the editors' concerns about the threats and their desire to talk to her more about what was going on. As if she knew. But she was used to working mostly remotely as a journalist, so even if she wasn't hiding out here in Chance, she wasn't going to just drop everything and hurry to those different publications' offices.

Unless, now, she had reason to believe she would learn more about those threats and their sources. But as far as she knew, that wouldn't happen if she decided to temporarily ignore that she had actually been accepted at this shelter as a staff member they were going to protect like the rest, whatever their reasons for being there.

And she hoped to find out some of those reasons with the people she had met, eventually. To satisfy her own curiosity. She wouldn't use any of it in an article. She'd promised Scott, and Bryson. And herself.

Okay, concentrate, she told herself. She read Wanda's emails yet again. And she decided to respond to the most recent one, nicely and apologetically, but without indicating where she was, and making it clear she had no plans now or in the future to go visit the *Pup Rescue Forever* offices. Never mind that those offices were in San Francisco and she was closer now, while in Chance, to that California city she really liked than when she was at home in LA.

Doing articles remotely for them still worked best, especially if she could avoid whatever threats were apparently showing up for her there as well as elsewhere, like Macie's *Puppies, Kittens and Humans*' San Diego offices.

Taking a deep breath, she finally began typing the response she'd been pondering:

Hi, Wanda. It's so good to hear from you, despite the circumstances. Yes, I saw your other emails too but I haven't had much access to my emails either on my phone or my computer, so I didn't respond in a timely manner. I'm really upset and concerned about the terrible correspondence you've been receiving about me and my stories, and still wish I knew what it was about. It's been happening recently in my emails and in what other editors receive. I'm so sorry, and I'm trying to figure it out. If you have any ideas, please let me know. Meantime, I'm continuing to research my next article for you and hope to be able to submit it soon. Unfortunately though, I won't be able to visit you in your office. Thanks so much for your kindness and patience. Harper.

Yes, definitely Harper now. She reread it a couple of times, then pressed Send.

She'd no idea when Wanda would respond to her, or if she would at all, considering how angry she'd sounded. Well, Harper could follow up in the next day or so if she didn't hear back, be friendly and try to stay in touch with this editor, at least. And hopefully others too, including

Macie, although she didn't think she'd seen any emails from Macie today.

For now, Harper went through the recent emails from Wanda again, then forwarded them to Bryson including her own response, letting him know she was about to open the other emails she'd received that day and would forward any difficult ones to him too, as they'd agreed.

She sat there for a few moments, glancing down at cute, sleeping Lorrie. Then she took another sip of water from her glass. And inhaled deeply before opening one of the email folders she kept on her computer, one where she stored the fan mail she had gotten.

Fortunately, she had a lot of fans, so a lot of emails were there. She didn't attempt to remember all the addresses or jot them down, but hoped she would recognize any that popped up in her current email list.

And, in fact, there were several. She opened them to help her mood become happier, at least for a moment. They mentioned several of her recent articles and some asked when she'd have more articles published and where.

She would definitely respond to them, but not right now.

Instead, she opened another email folder, one she wished wasn't there but where she saved the nasty emails and threats she had received. Oh, yes. She wanted to remember at least some of those addresses too, even though she wished those horrible critics, and worse, didn't exist.

She didn't open those emails now, at least, but just tried to file a few of the addresses in her mind.

Then she went back to her current emails.

Oh, yes, damn it. A couple of those addresses she'd just attempted to memorize were there.

She started opening them, trying not to cringe as she read them. She had a purpose, after all, besides wanting to see what they said. Yes, these, from the same senders, were nasty too, some threatening. Wanting to know when her next article would be. Asking if it would be better than the last ones, which they claimed were trash.

Some even demanded that she respond by saying where she was so the sender could meet with her in person with the specifics of the problems they noted, and deal with her. Physically.

So many of those…and she'd rarely received that kind of email before recently.

What was happening? Why? Who was involved?

How could she get them to stop?

Harper next forwarded the troubling emails to Bryson with a note that indicated these were people who'd already sent her threats, so these emails weren't the first from them.

She wondered what Bryson would think. He'd be angry, probably. And knowing him, determined to track at least some of them down and get them to stop. Maybe even figure out a way to get them arrested.

If only she'd said yes to Bryson and he was with her now, while she was going through this.

But he wasn't, and she had to continue.

In addition to forwarding those messages to Bryson, she stuck them in the same email folder where she'd saved the last ones.

And wished she had at least a glass of wine to help mush up her mind. But she didn't.

And it was time to start opening those emails she'd received that she hadn't yet read or identified.

Only... Well, first, it wouldn't hurt to open a few from those she recognized as fans. Although just then, considering her state of mind, she couldn't help wondering if at least some of them had hated something she'd recently published and written to her to let her know they were no longer fans. Or—

Okay. She needed to at least scan through a few and see if her concerns were at all justified—and if not, then allow herself to bask for a few moments in some good comments from readers who actually liked her.

She started with an email address she recognized, one used by a senior lady who apparently lived close to one of the shelters in LA's San Fernando Valley that Harper particularly liked. She dropped in there a lot to talk to the owners and their staff and volunteers, and interview them about how things were going at any particular time, most often when they held a major adoption event, which they held every few months. It was called Temporary Pet Home, and was promoted as bringing in a lot of new needy animals for anyone seeking a new family member.

Harper had used Temporary Pet Home as the subject of several fun and well-received articles.

Now, holding her breath, Harper opened that email. It was indeed from Babs, her fan, asking when the next article about Temporary Pet Home would be published, and in which publication, and saying she was about ready to adopt another dog and maybe Harper would want to write about that.

Oh, yes she would! If she could. She had met Babs in person a few times and liked the older woman a lot. And under other circumstances she'd want to be there when Babs met the latest adoptable bunch and picked out her own new baby.

But right now, Harper couldn't plan anything. At least not anything good.

She would definitely respond to Babs and find a way to be cheerful and encouraging, and even possibly ready to write an article as Babs suggested without being there to meet Babs's new baby, at least not immediately.

Okay, she had to stop being nice to herself. Time to go through the other emails. And hope that no more were threatening, but if so, she'd forward them to Bryson.

And either way, threats or not, she wasn't about to give up on her career. She had some ideas for new articles for these editors and possibly other magazines. She'd even begun researching a few, and she could continue with that remotely.

Now. Right now. And try to keep herself sane and still continuing with, and enjoying, the career she loved.

Fortunately, it didn't take Bryson much longer to finish eating dinner with Aunt Andrea and accompanying her to her apartment.

Damn, but he was worried about Harper. Yes, she was currently at the safest place he knew of, under official protection. And who knew how much she really needed? After all, those threats were sent mostly to her editors, sometimes to her, but nothing indicated who had sent them or why…except for not liking Harper's writing. Or what that person intended to do, if anything, besides send threatening emails to get the attention of Harper and her editors.

Still, she wisely wasn't ignoring them, and neither was he.

Kara had gotten the temporary license plate for Harper's car dropped off that day, and now Bryson had it in his possession.

He'd left Andrea's a few minutes ago and driven back to his condo. After parking, he'd gone inside and immediately booted up his computer.

And opened the first of Harper's emails. It was one she had forwarded from an editor, a different one from the person whose communications he had seen earlier.

This one was sent to editor Wanda Grey. The threat was nasty, but not as bad as the others. It emphasized more of the bad reviews that had been posted about one of Harper's articles in the publication *Pup Rescue Forever.*

It mentioned that the email's writer, who just called herself Lady Reader, had written one of those reviews. It, in effect, ordered the writer, Harper, to stop writing her nasty, untrue articles. Period. Or suffer the consequences.

Unspecified consequences, but even so...

When Bryson finished reading that one, he considered sending a response to Harper but checked his emails again first and saw she had forwarded a couple more. Those had also been forwarded by Wanda and included other emails and unpleasant reviews. And not only were they also threatening, but Wanda's responses to Harper also got nastier, demanding that Harper reply and do something about those reviews, and even show up at the *Pup Rescue Forever* offices to discuss it all with Wanda.

Even though Harper just forwarded these emails without comment, Bryson could imagine what she was thinking. They weren't the reason she had wanted to go into protection at the Chance Animal Shelter since they'd been sent while she was already there, but they certainly wouldn't make her feel any better, or any closer to wanting to get out of there and go home, which had to make being there a good thing right now.

As he finished reading all three emails from Wanda, he considered calling Harper but decided to look at his emails again. And there were four more Harper had forwarded.

He again opened them one at a time. For each, Harper introduced them by saying they were in her inbox. One had been sent via an address she recognized as being someone who had already sent her threatening messages. The other two were new senders.

And all three were nasty. They each indicated the senders thought Harper's media stories about animal shelters and dog rescues and wildlife observation were horribly researched and wrong in their results. And written badly enough that those senders, who, in their own ways, claimed to be animal aficionados, were not only going to post scathing reviews, but also wanted to know where Harper was so they could talk with her about her ending her writing...or else.

Nothing specific, but they implied her writing career wasn't the only thing they wanted to affect.

They wanted to stop her.

All were similar in that way to the threatening messages she had received before.

But why?

And who were these people?

Bryson could only hope that these weren't the only

emails Harper had received, and that some had been nice and friendly.

But either way…

He recognized he had something he needed to do that evening, even though he had to be at Barky Boulevard early the next morning, as he often was.

Right now, he made a call. As much as he wanted to talk to Harper though, and attempt to soothe her, he had a much better idea.

But he had to make certain it was alright.

And so he called Scott.

"Hi, Bryson. Everything okay?" the Chance Animal Shelter director asked immediately.

"Yes and no," Bryson responded, and told the man currently in charge of protecting Harper about those emails. "I'm glad you're letting her get online, for her career and otherwise, but this stuff sucks."

"Got it. Anything you want me to do right now?"

"Just one thing," Bryson responded.

Scott quickly agreed. And soon Bryson was driving to the Chance Animal Shelter…without getting Harper's okay.

He was driving his own car this time, another SUV. His was black. He'd left Harper's white one in a parking spot at his condo, where he had parked it before. He still needed to change the license plate.

Soon, he reached the shelter and parked in the shadows at the rear, in the same nearly empty lot where he'd last parked when he'd brought Harper here. He then headed once more not to the main entrance, but for the smaller door at the other end of the lot.

Then he called Scott again.

But it was Nella who opened the gate a minute later. "Thanks," Bryson told her.

There was a wry grin on her pretty face when she said, "I gather Mia isn't aware you were coming."

"I didn't want her to say no," he admitted.

Nella walked with him for only a short distance until he reached the downstairs lobby of the apartment building.

"Call me to let you out if she boots you out," Nella said, then headed toward the main office building.

"Will do," Bryson said, grinning back...though he was concerned she was right about what Harper/Mia's attitude would be.

After all, he was no longer her protector, at least not officially.

But he did head up the steps to the third floor, then knocked on Harper's door. And waited, though not very long.

The door opened. Harper looked out at him, her green eyes huge. Yes, Harper when they were alone together, unless she told him otherwise.

What was she thinking? What was she feeling?

"Bryson!" she exclaimed.

And he no longer worried about her possibly booting him out. She grabbed his arm and pulled him inside, and he had to be careful not to step on Lorrie, who was also right there.

"I wanted to make sure you were alright and feeling—" he began.

But he couldn't finish what he'd started to say. They were suddenly in each other's arms, lips on each other's, and kissing deeply and hotly.

Chapter 15

He was here. Harper had wished it, even though she'd told Bryson to stay away, that the protection here at the shelter was just fine.

But now, she couldn't be happier as they sat on the sofa in her small apartment's living room, talking as Lorrie stood on her hind legs demanding Bryson's attention.

They weren't kissing. Not now. But she'd not even thought about it when she'd pulled him inside the door and attacked him with her body, her lips. The feel of him against her had brought back memories of long ago, and not so long ago.

Dumb? Probably. But she was so stressed that having Bryson with her alleviated some of the fear and anger that had just been stoked here, while she was under official protection yet peeking at the world remotely and pondering a whole lot more.

"Just so you know," he told her as he scratched Lorrie behind the ears, "I'll contact Scott again while I'm here and see if they have an apartment where I can hang out some evenings while you're living at the shelter. I've visited often recently but haven't been assigned a place to stay overnight, and—"

"Hey, do you want me to get angry with you not only

for showing up here when I told you it wasn't a good idea, but also for not staying with me on those nights that you do happen to visit, now that you've come anyway?" She had moved away from him on the sofa and put her hands on her hips as she glowered at him, or at least pretended to. But she was smiling.

And so was he.

"Well, Scott is aware I'm here now, and I could just let him know that I'm hanging out in your place overnight, though I won't *necessarily* make it a habit."

Harper was glad to hear his emphasis of the word *necessarily*. That suggested that he might make it a habit anyway. Only—

Well, she didn't want to stay here forever, despite her relief at having been accepted at Chance Animal Shelter. For now, yes. Of course. But she wanted to clear things up in her life, get those threats resolved, or even make herself able to ignore them since she hadn't actually been attacked, and go back to being herself in her career. Never mind how stressed she'd felt over the latest threats.

Even if it once more meant not seeing Bryson again, or at least as often. But she would deal with that. Maybe fix it too, and maintain a relationship with him this time.

For now though, she just had to live with things, and if that included living with Bryson again some of the time just because he wanted to help keep her safe? Well, it would certainly keep her happy too.

Although the fact that he was such a kind and protective man, and one who didn't mind sharing a bed with her and more, didn't really resolve anything, not even between them.

After talking with him before, sharing those latest nasty emails, she'd had an idea. Well, not a new idea, but to try to clear her mind of the negative stuff she wanted to—what else?—write an article to submit to one of her editors. Maybe Macie. Maybe Wanda. Or how about Betsy Bordley, or even a different editor altogether? But whoever it was, she would make it clear she had researched the story a while ago, before all this began, because the subject of it would be Barky Boulevard.

She decided to tell Bryson about it before they took Lorrie out for her last short walk of the evening.

Looking at Bryson as they sat there, she said, "My mind has been on a lot of stuff lately, and one of the things I've thought about is how wonderful I think Barky Boulevard is. I'd like to write an article about that fun doggy day care center for one of my publications." She didn't exactly ask his permission, but if he was absolutely against it, she would argue with him but most likely back down.

But he was against her being put in further danger, such as by letting the world know she was in Chance.

"Not a good idea," he said. "It might make it appear you could be in Chance. Can't you write about other pet- or rescue-related places?"

"Of course, and I'll submit articles about a couple of them at the same time so as not to make my whereabouts obvious. And I'll indicate I researched this one a while ago. But—" Okay, she had to say it. "The thing is, if whoever it is does get the hint and come to Chance looking for me, maybe that person can finally be identified and caught. And I know it hasn't been too long since I've been in hiding, but I can't hide forever. I won't hide forever, despite the danger I could be in. So it might even be a good thing to hint about where I am, as long as Scott, Sherm and Kara and the rest of the local PD are kept aware of what's going on." *And you'll certainly be aware of it, cop-on-leave*, Harper thought.

"I don't like it," he said. "You ran away, came here, because of those concerns, and you've been accepted here at the shelter, but you already want to drop those protections and—"

"I don't want to drop them," she asserted. "And in fact, I want to utilize them as much as I can. But I want my real life back too, as fast as possible."

"But your real life recently has been full of those threats, and that person, or people, certainly sounds serious, considering the number and contents of the threats. Look, Harper, you came here looking for safety, and you've found it. Why jeopardize it all right away? Why don't you at least wait for a while before doing anything foolish like that?"

"Foolish? I'd consider it kind of brave, and definitely necessary for getting my real life back." She was standing now, glaring down at Bryson, her hands on her hips.

He rose too, and took her into his arms, and it felt good. Still…

"I understand," he said. "I really do. But I want you safe, here at the shelter out of harm's way, preferably until we figure out who's been threatening you. And I will work with the local cops to keep an eye out for anything amiss here, anyone who doesn't belong. And I assume you'll keep me informed about any additional threats, right?"

She nodded, her head now against his hard, muscular

chest. "Of course." But then she pulled back and looked into his face—his handsome face, with his dark brown eyes looking back down into hers. "But I need a plan. *We* need a plan. As much as I appreciate all you've done, and the fact I've been accepted here for my protection, I really need to figure out a way to learn where those threats are coming from. *Who* they're coming from. I haven't really talked to any staff members here about their lives or why they're in protection, but I assume they don't intend to spend the rest of their lives here either. And if they're in a kind of witness protection, maybe they'll be given new lives eventually, new identities and places to live and jobs and all. I don't want to wind up being someone different. Somewhere different from my former home would be fine, but once I'm gone from here I still want to be Harper Morsley, journalist, writing my animal-related articles. And I assume that can only happen if the source of my problems is identified and dealt with, and I intend to do all I can to ensure that happens." She paused, then smiled a little. "And I assume that's more likely to happen if I have your help."

"Well, I'd like to assume that too, but I'll be happy when you're truly safe, no matter how it happens. Now, I think it may be time to take your little Lorrie out again. Then we can head for bed."

What he said about going to bed wasn't suggestive really. He was just mentioning going to bed.

But she could still have her hopes.

And those hopes were realized a while later when they really did get into her bed here at the shelter, the first time for her and also for him in this one, she figured.

They kissed good-night, and she was delighted when his hands began exploring her body and the kisses turned into more.

Bryson definitely enjoyed the time before he fell asleep that night. At least the first part.

Their lovemaking was phenomenal, as usual. He remembered it well from before, as well as last night.

And when they were lying together afterward, he was glad Harper's breathing grew deep as she fell asleep, her soft, still bare curvaceous body snuggled against his.

At least one of them was relaxed, for now. But he kept thinking about what she'd said. She intended to maintain her career, sure. Even from here, and it had already been discussed with Scott. That was fine.

But her doing an article on Barky Boulevard? Under other circumstances, he would have liked the idea. Even though he hoped he'd be able to get things under control there enough that he could return to his life as a cop while still helping his aunt from a distance, he really cared about the doggy day care place and its employees, as well as the pups they took in to watch. And having it become more popular thanks to publicity, such as an article by Harper, sounded wonderful.

But not under the current circumstances.

Not unless he could help things improve for Harper. A lot. Enough that he would feel she was no longer in danger.

And that, as she'd recognized, would require figuring out who was doing this to her, and bringing them into custody.

Plus, he really hoped to learn why. Whoever it was

clearly had a grudge against Harper. Something to do with her writing, apparently.

Had she insulted the person or people? Done something else to undermine whoever they thought they were?

Well, thinking and worrying about it at the moment wouldn't resolve the situation. He settled even closer to Harper and allowed himself to fall asleep.

In the morning, she got out of bed before he did, throwing on some clothes including a shelter T-shirt. "Good morning," she said when he looked up at her. "Lorrie's awake. I'm taking her out."

"Good idea." Bryson rose quickly and also pulled on a shirt and jeans. He didn't stress too much about Harper going outside on her own with her dog here, but he liked the idea of staying in her company as much as possible.

There were already some staffers outside walking dogs, which wasn't a surprise to Bryson. And when Lorrie was done, they returned inside, and they both showered, Harper first.

Then it was time for breakfast. Bryson didn't spend the night here often, but enough to know the routine. Scott and Nella were already inside the cafeteria, as were some people Bryson recognized, and apparently Harper did too, since she said hi to Sara, as well as Kathy, Chessie and Leonard, who all sat together at one of the long tables. When Harper, with Lorrie leashed beside her as always, went to the food table to get a plate, Bryson lagged behind. He went over to say good morning to Scott.

"All okay?" the shelter director immediately asked, standing up near the table where he'd been eating beside Nella.

"Fine," Bryson responded. "And thanks again for accepting…Mia. Now, if she'll only settle down…"

"Has she been online working and checking her email and all that?"

"Yeah, and there have been more…difficult communications." Bryson kept his voice low.

"Not surprising, I guess. But keep me informed."

Which Bryson definitely would. Especially since he'd been pondering what Harper had suggested yesterday, and he just might go along with it.

As long as they could be careful.

Right now, he drew closer to Scott, to speak softly into the director's ear, and said, "I'm thinking about taking Harper downtown today for a quick visit to Barky. I know you're always on alert around here anyway, but it might help to be even more watchful. I'll let you know if anything comes up, like an indication she or Barky are being watched."

"Fine, but is it a good idea to take her away from here even for a short while?"

It probably wasn't, but again Bryson had been considering what Harper had said. He wouldn't want to overdo it, or allow her to, but maybe they'd come up with a way to figure out more about who was threatening her.

And being away from the shelter for a short time might help them get further ideas.

"It won't be long, and we'll be careful. I know she wants to write more articles while she's here, and featuring my doggy day care place sounds like a good idea as long as it doesn't become obvious she's here now. She said she'd mention she'd researched that one before, and she'll submit other articles to her editors at the same time that she's already researched at locations not around here. Oh, and yeah, she made it clear to me again that she'll get your approval before submitting any of them." Mine too, he hoped.

"Okay, then. Let me know when you're ready to leave and I'll make sure you both, and Lorrie, are let out properly. Also tell me when you expect to return, although you should call a few minutes before you're ready to come back in."

"Got it," Bryson said. "I think we'll want to leave in twenty minutes or so, but I'll confirm that with Mia and let you know." Yes, he knew how to continue to refer to Harper here at the shelter when speaking louder.

And, in fact, about twenty minutes later they were finished with breakfast. Bryson had already taken Mia aside from their table and told her the plan, and she seemed thrilled. "Oh, thank you so much!" The expression on her face suggested she wanted to kiss him again, but they still had the breakfast crowd around so they didn't get too close.

They hurried back to her apartment along with Lorrie, and Mia shoved her laptop into its backpack so she could type some notes for her story while they were at Barky Boulevard, though he made it clear they wouldn't be there for long.

He was also glad that she was going to research a story about the day care center rather than immediately focus on writing something about Chance Animal Shelter. At least her current real location wouldn't be as obvious that way, although her visiting Chance recently would be clear.

"Ready?" he asked as she headed for the door.

"Absolutely."

They were careful as they made their way to the parking lot door, wanting to appear they were just walking Lorrie. But Nella, who'd apparently been informed by Scott what they were up to, met them there and let them out.

Soon, they were in Bryson's car, going to Barky Boulevard. "Does your aunt expect us?" Harper—yes, she was Harper again—asked from the passenger seat.

"Andrea's aware I'm up to some other things in Chance, like visiting the shelter now and then to help out, but she's always happy when I show up to help at Barky. She isn't expecting me now, no, but I'm sure she'll be glad to have me there. You too. I assume you'll want to work with the employees and dogs a bit for your research."

She laughed. "You've got me pegged."

And that expression made him wish that he did have her pegged…again. But not this afternoon, and who knew when, if ever, again. Although he did intend to accompany her back to the shelter that evening. He could always hope…

They soon pulled into a parking space near Barky Boulevard, got out of the car and walked Lorrie briefly, and Bryson did act as himself and keep an eye on their surroundings, not that he knew what he was looking for. But would what Harper was up to now help him find the answer, and without endangering her further?

Oh, yeah. Even if they didn't sleep together that night, or again, he'd want to stay as close to Harper as possible to ensure her safety.

And he was happy, and amused, when, after they entered the doggy day care facility, Harper put the bag she was carrying into his office and approached Aunt Andrea. "Would it be okay if I helped to work with the dogs here today?"

Andrea nodded immediately, causing her long brown-and-gray hair, pulled partly back behind her head, to waft around her pretty but aging face. "That would be wonderful, Hanna, dear. And they can also help you work with your cute little Lorrie."

"Perfect!" And Harper/Hanna here was soon down on the floor with trainers Cindy and Ellie, along with dogs of various sizes, as usual, from Chihuahuas to Labrador retriever mixes and even another French bull who resembled Lorrie but was brown instead of black. Cindy took over working with Lorrie, who appeared to love it.

And Hanna? She threw balls and got dogs to fetch. She gave some simple commands as the workers there did, like "sit," "stay" and "come." She asked those other workers a lot of questions about their work here, and the dogs and their owners, and what made Barky Boulevard more special than other doggy day care places, besides it being the only one in Chance.

Bryson had thought she didn't plan to work with the pups and people this long, but he realized this was all part of her research and wondered how she would fit everything into her article, or how much of it she'd use.

And meanwhile, he wandered around Barky Boulevard and took walks outside to try to ensure all was well…and fortunately it appeared to be.

After nearly an hour, she finally rose and came over to where he'd just been watching from one of the chairs where dog owners could also rest and watch, and where a middle-aged woman and senior man had hung out for a while, cheering on their own pups, but now had left.

"Okay if I go rest for a while in your office?" she asked him. She was panting a little and had been working hard with a golden retriever mix just a few minutes before. Her beautiful face was flushed a bit beneath her wavy blond hair, and her green eyes looked really happy.

He figured she wanted to start writing her article, or at least make notes.

"Fine with me," he said. "Okay if we leave in about half an hour?" Would that give her enough time to accomplish what she wanted here?

"Sounds good," she responded, which pleased Bryson. He'd be able to take her back to the shelter and worry about her a little less for a while.

And maybe use her security as an excuse to stay the night again.

Chapter 16

They were back in her apartment, and Harper immediately sat down on one of the chairs facing her kitchen table, where she'd placed her laptop. She had told Bryson it was okay to watch TV in the living room as long as he kept the volume low.

She'd already typed preliminary notes about what she'd researched that day at Barky Boulevard, not that it was any different from the way she had worked with some of the employees and pups when she was there before as Hanna. But now, she knew she was going to write an article within the next day or so, and she made some mental notes about what she wanted to include. She entered them on the computer as a reminder and a prompt and an inspiration.

She then forced herself to check her emails. Nothing scary, fortunately. She had some calm messages from her regular editors, who'd apparently not received anything controversial about her for the moment, plus one from an editor she had written for before, but not recently. A couple of fan emails, which made her smile. Some spam, which she deleted.

She could relax somewhat. But she had work to do.

She started to write the article about Barky Boulevard,

and what a wonderful facility it was, even compared with others she had written about before and extolled. She mentioned the owner of Barky, Andrea Andell, without mentioning her name or the difficulties that had led to her nephew stepping in to help. Harper described being allowed to get down on the floor with the caretaker/trainers there and working with and playing with the dogs being cared for. She wrote about how enthusiastic and caring those employees were, also not mentioning them by name. She'd taken some pictures with her phone and figured she'd send them along with her article, but ones where only the facilities and dogs were depicted. No sense potentially endangering anyone, and it was unlikely that anyone threatening her would show up there anyway, let alone seek out a dog or two who'd happened to be there.

She wouldn't include any photos that had Lorrie in them even though her dog sometimes appeared in her articles, but that was before the threats had begun. Mentioning Lorrie shouldn't matter now, but she didn't want to put her dog out there at the moment, with all those threats coming in.

The short article didn't take her very long to write. She reread it twice and did a little editing. She kept the file open on her computer, though, when she sought out a couple more articles she had recently written though not yet submitted, both of which took place at locations far from Chance that were mentioned in the writing.

She reread both of those too, and was pleased with what she had written. She always liked to have extra articles available in case she was contacted by an editor who needed something quickly and Harper didn't have time to immediately drop everything she was doing and research a new story.

Like now.

She nevertheless read all three articles once again. And this time, she had an obligation to fulfill before sending them to editors for possible publication.

She also felt somewhat confused. Usually, she figured out pretty fast where to send a new story. But now, she wasn't sure how to handle the article that featured a location in Chance.

She would run all three stories by Bryson first, and if he was okay with them, she'd next ask Scott to approve them before she sent them out, as she'd told him she would.

But which one would she send, and where? Maybe the two men could make some suggestions as to how to handle this.

It was obvious whom to ask first. Harper made sure all three articles were open and accessible on her computer, then stood and walked into her living room.

Sure enough, Bryson was on the sofa, watching the TV mounted on the wall across from it. He'd done as she requested and kept the sound low, but had the news on.

Harper couldn't help wondering what was going on in the rest of the world. Not that she had been in Chance long, but it was a fairly isolated location, making it an ideal place for her to hang out, especially at this shelter.

"How's the world?" she asked him.

"Difficult as usual," he responded. "Shootings and fires and politics and all. How's your writing?"

"Well, I'd like your opinion on that." She explained she had three articles she was ready to show Scott, including one on Barky Boulevard. "I haven't quite figured out which editor to send which article," she continued. "I don't want to emphasize my visit here to Chance to any of them, even though I said in the article that it was in the past. I doubt any of them would publicize it, but I don't want to risk it. I'm considering sending a blurb out for each of those articles to my usual three editors, and let them know that's what I'm doing, to learn their reactions. They might all be too irritated with me, and my not focusing on them right now, and the reviews and threats and all, to publish any one of the articles. But if they like the ideas, maybe I can get them all published around the same time by negotiating who gets which one."

"Sounds like a good plan to me." Bryson rose. "I assume I should come into the kitchen to read the articles, right?"

"Right." It didn't take long to get there, but on the way Harper briefly described the other two articles. One was about a new veterinarian, Dr. Yolanda Jantis, who had only recently begun practicing in Anaheim, California, and had decided to focus half her practice on treating the pets of homeless people. She was far from the only one doing that, but brand-new at it and hadn't gotten as much publicity as many others so far, although fortunately she had donors who helped her manage the costs.

The other was about a pet shelter in San Francisco that took in as many dogs as it could from other nearby shelters who hadn't found homes in many months of living there, sometimes because of size, sometimes behavior, sometimes even obvious disfigurements such as lack of legs or eyes. And it'd had good success in finding most of them homes.

Harper figured the editors would find the articles interesting—the other two possibly even more interesting than the one on Barky Boulevard. And they all took place in different parts of California, so it wouldn't be obvious where Harper was, although where she had gone previously for her research would be clear.

But would they consider them interesting enough to publish? Hopefully. And also hopefully, Harper would figure out the best way to determine which publication got which article this time. She was well aware of how much each of them paid for their articles and would be happy whichever way they went.

When Bryson and she sat down, Harper first brought up—what else?—the article about Barky Boulevard. She said nothing while Bryson read it, although she watched his face, and was pleased when his smile kept broadening.

"This is really good," he said in a few minutes. "I like how you dealt with Andrea and the unnamed employees and definitely the dogs and your working with them. And you indicated in the article that you researched it some time ago, so it won't be obvious you're still in the area. You definitely have my approval."

"Thanks." And Harper felt so good she couldn't resist sharing a kiss with him.

He liked the other articles too, and commented about both after he read them. And, yes, Harper used his nice critiques as a reason to kiss him yet again.

"Okay for me to run these by Scott now?" she finally asked. "There's nothing at all about Chance Animal Shelter, so hopefully he'll okay all of them too."

"I figure," Bryson said. "Go for it. While you send them, I'll text him to let him know they're on their way."

Harper attached all three articles to an email to Scott and pressed Send fairly quickly. And now, she'd have to wait to get his opinion.

Would he have time to look at them soon, or would it take a while?

Bryson must have sensed her concern over timing since he told her, "Maybe we should go outside with Lorrie for a little while, in case—" His phone made a sound that interrupted him. "It's a response text from Scott," he said after glancing at it, and opened it. "He's fortunately in his office and said he'd read them now. Meantime, we can still take Lorrie for a walk."

"Sounds good to me," Harper responded. At least this way she'd be able to think more about her pup than worry about what Scott's opinion would be, at least for a little while.

Outside, they walked Lorrie briefly, then Harper—Mia, out here—joined young, blond Chessie on the shelter's center walkway, where she was waving her thin arms and giving commands, and treats, to Moe, the black Lab mix. When they got close, Mia gave Lorrie similar commands and also got some treats for her from Chessie, who smiled and seemed pleased to have the company.

But Mia was highly concerned a few minutes later when she saw Scott leave the main building a short distance away and start walking toward them.

Was he about to give her bad news about her articles? Take her aside and scold her for things she'd included that he believed she shouldn't have?

He seemed to be heading toward them, and Chessie

said, "Uh-oh. Here comes our master. Are we in trouble?" But she was smiling, clearly not worried, though Mia was.

"Oh, good," Bryson said, coming up beside Mia and looking in the same direction she was. He gestured for her to follow him, and they moved a few feet away from Chessie. "I'll bet Scott has finished reading the things we asked him to."

Even though they weren't as close to Chessie now, Mia was glad Bryson wasn't any more specific. "Maybe," she responded.

Scott, in his usual Chance Animal Shelter work shirt, soon joined them. "Hey, Mia, come over here for a second, okay?" He gestured toward the nearest shelter building, where the medium-sized dogs were housed.

"Sure," she said as brightly as she could. She shot a quick, apologetic glance toward Chessie, who was grinning broadly. Then she gently pulled Lorrie in the direction she was now headed, though the pup resisted a little this time. Fortunately, she was easily directed with the harness she wore.

Harper was aware that Bryson joined them on the paving outside the building, and Scott soon turned his back toward where Chessie worked with Moe, and a few other staff members were now joining her.

Scott gestured for Mia to follow him a short distance away, then spoke in a low voice. "I read your articles, and they look fine—certainly nothing that would give away what this shelter is about or that you're here, since you didn't even mention it. Maybe someday you can, but I'm really glad you didn't now. So as far as I'm concerned, you can go ahead and send these out to get published.

And I appreciate our new system for me to check out your writing while you're one of our staff members."

"And I appreciate your approval and comments," Mia said, relieved. "I'll go inside now and do just that—send these articles out for, hopefully, publication. Thanks!" She'd figure out which magazines to send them to. With a glance toward Bryson, she pulled gently on the leash she held. "Lorrie, come."

The three of them walked toward the apartment building, passing a few other staff members who'd come out of the shelter areas with leashed dogs, including Leonard and Kathy.

Bryson accompanied Mia and Lorrie to the apartment upstairs. "You two okay here for a while on your own? I gather you'll be on your computer anyway, and I want to walk around the shelter, maybe with Scott, to make sure all's in order, the way I usually do when I visit here."

"Sounds fine with me," Harper said, now able to return to her real identity. She hoped it would be fine. Her state of mind remained in flux. She was happy that Scott had no problem with her articles, even though she'd figured he wouldn't, not with these. But she was about to contact the outside world again. Her editors, who'd been her friends and hopefully still were, despite all that had been happening.

But she still remained uncertain about the best way to handle sending out the articles.

Well, time to figure that out, especially since Bryson left again fairly quickly.

She did as she'd already decided, first sending emails to her main editors, Macie, Wanda and Betsy, telling them she was in a bit of a quandary. She'd written three articles she really liked but had several publications in mind, and could she send each of them at least a description of all three and figure out who liked which one best? She'd decide then whom to actually submit each to for publication, and then make sure whomever she chose for each one was okay with publishing it.

She admitted that this was an odd way to do this, but she was on the road researching a couple more stories and found this the easiest way to handle the situation.

Definitely an odd way to approach it. She knew that, even if she hadn't mentioned it to the editors. But it wouldn't give away when she'd researched each article, or her location at the moment. And that was important, as was maintaining her career and getting more articles published, hopefully all of these.

And under other circumstances, she would contact each of them with a phone call. But she didn't want to get into any detailed discussions right now, so she indicated she was busy researching a new article and wouldn't be able to get away to talk, though emailing should work.

She sent those three emails out and wished for immediate replies, but, of course, knew better. For now, she decided not to take Lorrie out again for a while, but instead dug into her online files of remaining ideas, considering what to work on next.

She didn't hear from any of those editors until the next day after breakfast, when she returned to her apartment before joining the staff members for the morning's doggy play-and-training routine, which she was now obligated to do and looked forward to.

Betsy was first. She sounded excited about the articles but grumpy about the way Harper was handling this.

"Unprofessional," she called it, but nevertheless said her favorites, in order, were the ideas about the doggy day care, the veterinarian and the special shelter.

Macie was next, only she was more than grumpy. She sounded angry and said that, though she liked the ideas, she definitely would not choose any new articles that way.

When you're ready to write again for Puppies, Kittens and Humans, contact me and I'll call you back so we can go through ideas together first, as we always do.

It made sense, but it would be a while before Harper was likely to have her next article published by *Puppies, Kittens and Humans.*

But fortunately, Wanda seemed alright, and her favorite idea was the one on the veterinarian. Decision made.

Harper would hopefully have two new articles published soon—within the next week online, depending on how much editing was needed, if any. The print versions would take longer. She knew what each publication would pay for her articles and should receive the generous funds in her bank account soon.

And her career was continuing, even while in hiding.

Days passed. Bryson felt frustrated.

Oh, not entirely.

It was a week after he'd first stayed overnight with Harper in her small apartment at the shelter, and he now continued to do so at night. For her ongoing extra protection, he confirmed with Scott, who often grinned at him, most likely figuring how they spent their nights.

But Bryson nevertheless felt better about Harper's safety if he stayed with her, even though she'd not received any further threats for a while. He'd like to think that what had happened before was just someone's stupidity, and that the someone now regretted it and had backed off forever.

Yeah, he'd like to think that. He did hope that, but it would just be too easy, and he didn't believe things in life were ever that easy.

He was glad Scott and he had read the articles Harper had wanted to submit to publications. No issues there. Harper had apparently worked with two editors about a couple of the stories she'd given Scott and him to read, and they'd just been published in the online versions of the publications, and one was the article about Barky Boulevard. She'd shown him the online magazine called *Pets and Love* and scanned through it until the article he was interested in appeared.

It looked good, and he hoped to get a print copy whenever it became available.

He felt glad the Chance Animal Shelter was a safe, well-secured location, in case Harper's harasser was just biding their time until the next nasty threat, possibly one they followed up on.

Still, he couldn't spend much time during the days at the shelter. Andrea clearly needed help with Barky's finances, or at least keeping track of her mortgage for the facility's building, her income from the people who brought their pets in and payments to the employees— the basics for running a business. She had done okay with it for years, but as laws were modified regarding taxes and she aged a bit, she just got more confused. Taking care of dogs and working with the employees were her real skills, but not taking care of money.

He might have been able to find her a good financial consultant, but for now he, half owner of the business, was an even better consultant.

Which was how Bryson spent a good deal of his time when at Barky, in his office there, dealing with business matters.

And when he had free time on the computer, he did what he had done quite a bit before, even after Harper and he had broken up. He checked on her published articles...and now, what reviewers had to say about them.

The new articles seemed well received, at least. There were several positive reviews, and it felt good to see what the reviewers said about Barky Boulevard and the article that described it so well.

When out of his office, he also worked with the dogs at Barky Boulevard along with Andrea and the employees. And though he realized it wasn't a good idea, he gave in to Harper's pleas every couple of days and brought her along with him for a while. Although he also watched her work with the animals at the shelter and the staff members sometimes, and she obviously enjoyed that too, she made it clear that she preferred not being at the shelter 24/7. And though she wasn't going to write another article about Barky, so what she was doing wasn't research for that, she might have been making mental notes that she perhaps could use someday in a story that was more generally about doggy day care than about Barky Boulevard.

And she wasn't Mia at Barky, she was Hanna, and

not Harper Morsley. Her identity wasn't obvious, in case anyone was looking for her in Chance, and there'd been no indication of that even after the article about Barky appeared online, fortunately.

Of course, Bryson continued stewing about the possibility, but the story had indicated the research was done a few months ago. Whoever was threatening her might believe she could be there, sure, but it was just as likely she was in Anaheim, where the article about the kind vet who took care of pets of the homeless people, or at other locations where her most recent articles were centered, or even near her home in Los Angeles.

It seemed like no time at all when nearly two weeks had passed since he'd read Harper's articles. Not that the timing mattered, but for some reason he was getting more worried again.

Or was that simply who he was? Nothing much had happened during that time. He liked helping his aunt, sure. And it was certainly an added bonus that he was also with Harper a lot of the time.

Dinner that Friday night seemed as enjoyable as always. Harper—Mia—and he had received the coveted invitation to eat at the same table as Scott and Nella. The staff members who ate with them varied, and were often the same people Mia worked with most during the day, along with Lorrie, to help exercise and train the sheltered dogs.

Tonight they included Kathy, Chessie and Leonard, but also some relative newcomers at the shelter, Jerry and Veronica.

Jerry, or whatever his real name was, was a middle-aged guy with a large, bald head and small, sad eyes.

Bryson gathered that he had been fairly well-to-do, but his kids had not only somehow stolen his wealth, but had seemed to threatened his life if he attempted to get that money back. As much as he hated fearing his own children, he had no way of proving those threats and had run away.

And Veronica also had problems with her family, mostly her stepkids, who'd gotten her husband to try to take over what little money she had—take it over the easy way for them, by killing her. She was in her forties and petite, so she might not have been able to fight them off, and she too couldn't prove their threats. And so she had left, fortunately finding the Chance Animal Shelter.

In any case, despite hearing a hint of those sad tales, Bryson enjoyed dinner that night, and it appeared Mia enjoyed it too. It didn't hurt that all the people around them frequently said nice things about Lorrie, who, of course, remained with her.

And when dinner was over and they returned to Mia's apartment, Bryson felt relaxed. Sort of.

Maybe.

And Mia—Harper again while they were alone together once more—seemed to be having the same kind of emotions.

"Tonight was fun as always around here," she said as he locked the door behind them. They were immediately in each other's arms, kissing heatedly and wonderfully. It was still a bit early for them to go to bed, but Bryson couldn't help being hopeful.

"I agree," he said against her lips.

"So why do I feel it's about time for something to go wrong?" Harper pulled back and looked at him quizzically with her beautiful green eyes. "I mean, I'd love to just forget why I'm here and finally leave, since the threats seem to be over. But are they?"

"I'd like to think so too," he told her, pulling her back into his arms. "But I'm too pessimistic to think that's true. Something's going to happen, or at least I feel that way. I'd like to think it won't, but—"

"I'm sure you're right," she said hoarsely against his chest. "I just wish I knew what, and when."

And so did Bryson.

Chapter 17

Time seemed to be passing so quickly…and so slowly too. Harper couldn't help being happy that she was here, enjoying her time at the Chance Animal Shelter, including her interactions with the sheltered animals and staff members, as well as her visits to Barky Boulevard every couple of days.

And even happier about the time she was spending with Bryson. They were close once more, but a lot of that was because he was taking care of her.

Once they knew she was truly safe, she would get back to her real life, and Bryson to his. Would they have a relationship then? She could hope, but things were so much in flux she just didn't know.

Right now, late morning in her shelter apartment, she did what work she could at her computer on the kitchen table. It was hard to research new articles from here, but she was at least coming up with ideas and looking up possible sources and locations.

Which was a good thing.

Even better for the moment was that the reviews of the two recent articles she'd gotten published were all really positive, or at least those she'd seen. The editors seemed really pleased too, and didn't send links to her with any-thing bad, only good ones.

"I love hearing about the best doggy day care cen-ters," said one post from a reader whose name Harper recognized from other good reviews in the past, along with more similar compliments.

And even more good things were said about the vet-erinarian, Dr. Yolanda Jantis, who was the subject of Harper's article published in Wanda Grey's *Pup Rescue Forever*. Wanda was in touch via email to make sure Harper had seen them, and Harper responded with a big thank-you.

In her emails, she questioned both editors on their thoughts about articles from her in the future, without any specifics as to when they wanted to publish some-thing or the next subject, although they'd all involve ani-mals, as always. Both seemed highly willing to publish more from her, as long as they found whatever articles she sent as acceptable as those in the past, like these new ones. They'd worked with her enough to know she'd co-operate in their editorial process.

And then there were her emails with Macie, who now indicated she might be interested after all in the article on that special shelter Harper had described to her. She asked her to send the entire story along now, then said she'd want to discuss it by phone once she'd read it.

Harper wished she could call her. They'd spoken on the phone about articles a lot previously. But at the mo-ment, that didn't sound like a good idea, since Harper wasn't talking to anyone by phone right now except Bryson. She didn't say no though, but sent the article along, crossing her fingers that Macie would like it well enough to just accept it as it was, or ask for only minor changes via email.

"It's almost time to go downstairs for lunch," Harper said, looking away from her computer and down at the kitchen's tile floor, where Lorrie was lying at her feet.

Her dog's big brown eyes opened, and she suddenly sat up as if she understood what her mama had said.

Harper laughed, and as she'd been doing each time she prepared to leave her work here, she checked her email once more before putting her computer into sleep mode.

She told herself she just wanted to read one more fan email for now but recognized that she was waiting for the next shoe to drop. Rather, she was waiting for the next critical, or threatening, email to pounce on her email account.

It had been a while since she'd received any. She kept thinking maybe she really could finally go back to her normal life, but she relied on Scott, and even more, Bryson, to okay it, and even now, when all seemed so much better, they both kept telling her to wait.

Obviously, they were waiting for that unwanted shoe as well, and most likely expecting it.

Of course, she appreciated their protectiveness, but when could she actually believe the bad stuff was finally in her past?

Ever?

But those men, experienced in law enforcement, knew best. Maybe one or both of them had seen the kind of nasty follow-up to danger that they, and she, feared. And so she would continue to obey them.

This time, when she checked her email again, as always holding her breath a few seconds, anticipating the next threat, another email from Macie had arrived.

We'd like to publish your article, she said. That special shelter you described sounds wonderful. I ran your article by Sally, and she really liked it too. And Harper saw that Macie had cc'd her boss, Sally Effling, the publisher and editor of *Puppies, Kittens and Humans*.

Which made Harper smile. A lot. And relax and breathe again. She'd always gotten along well with Sally, who had consistently seemed to like her writing and want more. Apparently, she did now too. She'd once even suggested hiring Harper.

Harper continued to enjoy the idea of remaining versatile and writing articles for multiple publications, but having Sally become her boss someday, as well as Macie's, tempted her although she'd still want to work remotely. She didn't want to move to San Diego, even when she left Chance.

Back to LA? Probably, unless it somehow seemed dangerous after all the threats she'd gotten, since whoever had been doing it might be able to track her down at her old location most easily.

She most likely wouldn't get a real job offer from Sally if she didn't move to San Diego, and that was fine. But Harper would remain open to new approaches, new beginnings, in her career.

Once she could do something about them.

For now, she finally closed down her computer and got Lorrie's leash. Time for a short walk and maybe a short session with some of the other staff members to work with, and help train, the pups who were here waiting for their new homes. And then lunch, and possibly staying inside afterward.

She, like the other staffers, couldn't be wandering outside when potential adopters came to the shelter, since for their protection they couldn't be seen by outsiders. So far, since she'd been here, those visitors had mostly come when Bryson had taken her briefly to Barky Boulevard, so she hadn't had to worry about it.

So what would this afternoon be like?

As she let Lorrie walk and sniff, they were joined by Chessie and Veronica.

And then, surprisingly, by Bryson, who was being accompanied by Scott.

"Interested in a short visit to Barky Boulevard this afternoon, after lunch?" Bryson asked.

"Absolutely," Harper—no, Mia, as always, out here, she reminded herself—responded. She glanced at Scott to make sure he was okay with it. After all, he was her chief protector as long as she remained a Chance Animal Shelter staff member.

He recognized why she was looking at him and smiled. "Yes, I'm here with Bryson at his request so I can confirm I'm okay with your afternoon expedition. Unless, of course, there have been any issues you haven't told me about yet." His dark eyebrows furrowed over his blue eyes as his arms folded across his chest. Did he have many staff members here who lied to him, or at least didn't tell him the whole truth?

That definitely wasn't Mia.

"No threats or difficult emails," she said, "or I definitely would have followed protocol and let you know."

His difficult expression transformed into a smile, and

Mia figured he'd just been doing his job as director here, but didn't really think she'd been holding anything back.

They did get in about a half hour of shelter dog training before lunch, and Mia got to work with the gray poodle Ashy, along with Leonard, who also worked with Lorrie a bit.

Then lunch in the large and friendly cafeteria, sitting at the table with Scott and Nella, as usual these days, as well as some of the staff members Mia liked best, although she hadn't met any she disliked.

But lunch couldn't go fast enough. As much as she liked the shelter, she was ready for a visit outside it, no matter how short. Besides, she liked hanging out at Barky Boulevard and working with those dogs too, when she could.

Soon, she was in Bryson's car again, with him driving and Lorrie fastened safely in the back seat. After they parked in their usual area, they did their next usual thing and let Lorrie walk on her leash for a few minutes before going inside the doggy day care center.

It was crowded, even more crowded than before the article had been published. Which clearly made Andrea thrilled, since she kept talking about it with Bryson, and with Hanna/Harper too. She didn't understand the whole situation, although she was aware that Hanna had researched the article, but supposedly sent the information off to her friend Harper Morsley to write as if she had been there instead.

Harper knew Bryson trusted his aunt despite the difficulties she'd gotten herself into, but the fewer people who knew the truth about her and her identity, the better.

Today though, Andrea seemed upset when Bryson

and Hanna arrived. She motioned for her nephew to join her in her office while Hanna, with Lorrie, joined the current shift of employees, who were playing with, and training, the large group of pups present for day care.

And Hanna couldn't help wondering what was going on.

"Everything okay, Andrea?" Bryson asked his aunt as she shut the door behind them quickly.

"No," she said, putting her hands up to cover her face so her graying hair splayed out around her fingers, alarming Bryson, who was often concerned about his aunt's state of mind.

"What—" he began, but she cut in, moving her hands to her sides as she spoke, her expression miserable.

"I liked the idea of that article about our day care center, letting the world know about us even here in small Chance," she began. "And we got such nice feedback from our local customers, and even more dogs were brought in. Everyone seemed happy. I certainly was. But—but this morning, when I checked my emails, there was one that was just horrible."

Uh-oh, Bryson thought. He immediately figured it might be something related to those Harper had previously received.

But was that person now trying to find other ways to harm Harper, or the subjects of her articles?

"I'm really sorry," he said, trying to soothe Andrea. "Please let me see it."

She motioned for him to follow her. She sat down at her desk chair and got on her computer, pressing some of the keys. Then she got up again. "Here's that email." Her voice sounded choked.

"Thanks," he said, wanting to slug whoever had sent it. And it was just as nasty as he anticipated. It even addressed Andrea by name, though she hadn't been mentioned in the article. The email said that the way Barky Boulevard was depicted in that recent magazine article might get them a lot more business, but with all the dogs of different sizes and the inexperienced trainers and all, the place was clearly a bad spot for people to bring their beloved pets and it should be shut down. It concluded that word would soon get out to the world about its problems.

"Damn," Bryson muttered before he forwarded that malicious, cruel email to himself, closed it and rose again. He took Andrea, who had been looking over his shoulder, into his arms. "You know that's all wrong. We take really good care of the dogs, and even our less experienced employees work hard to keep them all happy and safe." He paused. "Those kinds of communications happen though, thanks to nasty people out there who have nothing better to do with their lives than try to hurt others. But we'll watch out for anything like what they threatened and make sure people know the truth, that Barky Boulevard is as wonderful a doggy day care place as it's depicted in the article. Okay?"

"Okay," Andrea said softly. "And…well, I know you, Bryson. I'm sure you'll take care of it."

"I definitely will," he said. And hoped he could.

First, he wanted to let Harper know about that email. Not that she would be happy, but she should be aware of it. Even though not directed at her, it was a bit threatening about her writing, maybe the next step from the person who'd been so horrible to her.

Andrea and he left her office, and he was glad to see a couple at the entry area with a leashed border collie with them, most likely wanting to leave their dog for a visit. Good. Andrea went over to greet them.

Bryson scanned the crowd and saw Harper—Hanna, here—in a corner with another of the employees, plus Lorrie and two other dogs, small ones, a Chihuahua mix and a Yorkie, working with them on commands, clearly a "sit and stay."

He was relieved to see one of the Barky people with her, since he approached and waited to catch her attention. He gestured with his head for her to join him and was glad when she immediately said something to the other person in that group.

She was beside him in just a couple of minutes. "Everything okay?" she asked. He figured his concern must have been evident on his face.

"There's something that just came up that I need to tell you," he responded, and now she looked worried too. As she probably should.

They went into his office, Lorrie at Harper's side, and she asked what was wrong. "I'll show you," he said. This time, rather than using her laptop, which she'd left in its bag in a corner, they sat at his desk and got on his laptop…and he soon showed her the email Andrea had received that he'd forwarded to himself. "Not sure whether this is anything to worry about except maybe some competing doggy day care around here, but I figured you'd better see it, just in case."

She gasped in dismay. "Oh, no. It's not a threat, and

I, of course, see other criticisms of my stories, but… I think I'll check my own email."

She stood again, got her own computer out of its case, plugged it in and sat back down beside him.

He watched as she scrolled through her emails, wishing he didn't have to be nosy but wanting to check for anything suspicious. He didn't recognize most of the names, which was fine. And Harper seemed okay as she checked to see the sources, some of which were probably spam, he figured.

She stopped at one though. "I'm not too concerned about any of them," she said, "But I suspect I'd better check this one. It's from Wanda Grey, my editor at *Pup Rescue Forever*. That's the one where my other recent article about the veterinarian was recently published." She opened it, and gasped again.

Bryson read over her shoulder. That editor had written to let her know about an email she had recently received about the story. It sounded very much like the one Andrea had just gotten regarding the article on Barky Boulevard.

"Looks like your menace is back at it," Bryson said. "Maybe not threatening you directly, but saying nasty stuff about what you've written to the subjects of those stories."

"Yeah," Harper said, her voice raspy. "I'll get in touch with Wanda now." She paused, then said, "And I wonder what's next."

Chapter 18

Bryson left his office then, letting Harper know he was going to go out and work with the dogs, and hopefully help to calm his aunt once more.

"That's fine," Harper said. At least she knew he would be nearby.

And she had to deal with this herself.

As soon as he left, shutting the door behind him, Harper bent down to pat Lorrie's head, then, with a sigh, returned to the computer.

The email from Wanda was highly disturbing to Harper, especially after seeing the one Andrea had received. Wanda indicated she'd only heard yesterday from Dr. Yolanda Jantis, the veterinarian who was the subject of Harper's recent article in *Pup Rescue Forever*. And Wanda was clearly upset about their communication and the reason for it: the vet's angry response about a nasty contact from a reader of the magazine who'd insulted the vet directly in an email to her, and not on a social-media site or by a review or otherwise, for what the article indicated she was doing.

Harper was a little surprised that Dr. Jantis hadn't contacted her since they had been in close touch previously when Harper was researching the article and had visited to see how the vet worked with the pets of her local homeless folks. Harper and Yolanda had exchanged emails, as well as phone calls. Not that Harper would have turned on her phone now and answered it, but she'd at least have known there'd been a call when she did check it. She hadn't seen any indication of communication by Yolanda, so maybe the veterinarian was so angry she didn't even want to contact Harper, but just got in touch with the obvious source of the publicity she had received, the magazine.

Still, one mean communication wasn't so bad, was it? Didn't Yolanda receive criticism sometimes in other ways?

Right now, Harper wished she felt comfortable making phone calls, hopefully to soothe one of her favorite editors, but, even more, to discuss this difficult situation with the veterinarian who had impressed her so much.

For the time being, though, she still wouldn't disobey the directives of Bryson and Scott and turn on her phone to contact anyone.

She started with a return email to Wanda, expressing her concern and likening this situation to the nasty reviews and threats that had occurred weeks ago. I don't know if they're related, Harper typed, but I wouldn't be surprised. In any case, I apologize to you, and I'll do the same with Dr. Jantis. As you could undoubtedly tell, I really thought what she does is fantastic and attempted to portray it that way, and believe I did. The fact one reader didn't like it and let Dr. Jantis know…at least I haven't seen any bad review that person might have posted, have you? She suspected Wanda's answer to that question would be negative in her response email.

Harper soon reread hers, made some small modifications, then sent it.

Then she wrote a similar apologetic email to Yolanda, and explained that the person who sent the original nasty email could be the same person who'd recently been really criticizing Harper and what she wrote, including some of the subjects of her articles. She didn't mention the threats though. And she told Yolanda once more how very much she appreciated and respected everything the vet did, and had attempted to convey that, above all, in her article.

After sending that email, Harper just sat for a while, staring at her now-blank computer screen. No actual threats had been received for now, and yet, with these awful communications about her most recent articles, she worried once more that her career, at least, was threatened.

And her, physically? Who knew, especially if the same person was at it again.

Harper felt no closer to figuring out who it was, or the reason for all the nastiness that had made her wonder before, and even more again now, the reason for it.

She'd really had enough. As much as she appreciated everything being done for her here, and as much as she appreciated Bryson's care and protectiveness in particular, she wanted her life back.

But she hadn't yet decided on a way to make that person, or people, show themselves and give her an opportunity to make them stop.

She had to determine what to do next.

But what would it be?

For now, she would get off her computer and go into

Barky Boulevard with Lorrie to play with the shelter dogs, and the staff members, for the rest of the afternoon.

Her frustration didn't ease up though, then or over the next few days.

Oh, yes, she recognized she had settled into a routine here. Most parts of her days, and all of her nights, were spent at the shelter. Fortunately, she was with Bryson, who clearly remained concerned but went back to his own life a lot during the days, or at least his current one. She realized, from what he said and didn't say, that he missed being a cop. But he was glad to be helping his aunt.

And her.

And she continued to appreciate that, and him, and her fairly safe life here, as well as her sometimes visits to Barky Boulevard.

She enjoyed her obligations as a shelter staff member and threw herself into working with the people and animals.

When she could, she got logged on to her computer and communicated more with her editors. At least the couple who'd been angry seemed to have settled down, since there'd been no further nasty communications about or reviews of her articles.

One good thing was that Macie had sent her the publication date for her article in *Puppies, Kittens and Humans* about that very special shelter that took in animals that other shelters were ready to supposedly euthanize, but there would have been nothing humane about those deaths. Harper was proud of that article and her prior visit to that shelter, so she felt good that it was finally going to be published.

She told Macie so in an email, cc'ing the publisher,

Sally Effling, since Macie had been doing the same thing recently. I'm really looking forward to seeing my article published in your wonderful magazine in a few days, she said in the email.

Me too, Macie responded in her follow-up email. Now I want to discuss with you what can come next. Do you have any other ideas? Are you researching anything now that could work for us?

I definitely have some great ideas, Harper replied, exaggerating a bit. Ideas, yes. Great? Well, they'd be greater if she could get on the road to the locations she had in mind to do her research, but that wasn't going to happen. Not now, at least.

And she hated stewing about when, even though that remained on her mind a lot.

I want to hear about those ideas, was Macie's reply. When can we schedule at least a conversation, if you can't visit here?

Never, immediately came to Harper's mind. Well, at least not in the foreseeable future. But all she said was Sorry, but with the traveling I'm doing now I just can't work in a phone call or a visit. Let's keep up our emails.

No response from Macie then, or for the next half hour while Harper remained on her computer.

She'd had enough emailing for the rest of that day, and she was glad, while working with Chessie and Leonard with a couple of the shelter dogs outside near the walkway that afternoon, to see Bryson return.

He joined them and also helped to train a couple of newcomer pups, including a border collie mix and another moderate size dog that Harper—yes, Mia now—couldn't determine the background of.

When it came close to dinnertime, those staffers joined a group of others who'd been working with dogs at the far end of the shelter pathway, and they headed toward the cafeteria.

"You hungry?" Mia asked Bryson.

"Sure." And the rest of their evening was spent with the usual crowd, including Scott and Nella.

Oh, yes, she liked it here. Appreciated it.

Appreciated Bryson, who, as usual, joined her in her apartment for the night. And she definitely had an enjoyable time with him before they fell asleep, which also was nearly usual these days.

But as Harper was lying in bed beside him, she wondered yet again how long this would last.

When would her real life return?

Could she make it actually return just by leaving here and going back to it?

She wasn't ready to find out how things would be if she simply left and became herself again, at least not yet, while those threats still floated in her mind.

Maybe she could finally do an article on the Chance Animal Shelter—only the animal part, of course—and tell her editors she researched it ages ago but was only just now writing it.

But would she feel confident that whoever was after her wouldn't follow up on that story and figure out what really was going on here?

She didn't want to find out. After all, it wouldn't only be her who'd be harmed if things went bad.

At least the next day was one when Bryson invited her to go to Barky Boulevard for a short while in the afternoon. They, of course, approached Scott first, in his office after breakfast this time, for his okay.

Which he fortunately gave.

And Harper, about to become Hanna for the afternoon, happily exited with Bryson and Lorrie into the parking lot, then into Bryson's car.

"It feels good to be out here again," she said to the man who'd been sharing her life so much. She definitely cared for him again. Even more than when they'd had a relationship before.

But she worried if that was just because she relied on him so much now.

Did they have a future?

Heck, that might depend on whether *she* had a real future.

"I'm sure it does," he said, a grin on his handsome face as he glanced at her from the driver's side, and Harper resisted the urge to lean over and kiss him.

They soon reached the other parking area Harper knew, near Barky Boulevard. She glanced around them as she exited the car, seeing that Bryson did his usual survey of the area, probably for her safety.

She got Lorrie out of the back seat and let her walk around for a few minutes before they headed into Barky's.

As they approached the front door, someone walked out, a tall lady wearing a wide-brimmed hat, and sunglasses despite having just been inside, and boots with high heels. Her dark hair was pulled into a ponytail. She didn't have a dog with her, so Harper—no, now she was Hanna once again—figured she had left her pup there for care that afternoon.

Something about the woman seemed familiar to Hanna/

Harper, so she decided she had seen her come or go with her dog on at least one of the occasions Hanna had been helping out there.

The woman glanced in their direction and turned, hurrying down the street. Hanna wondered why she seemed in such a rush, and what her reason was for leaving her dog there that day...

She wanted to find out more, most likely because of who she was those days, worried about everything and everyone around her.

"Are you okay?" Bryson asked from beside her, startling her. Her concern must be showing. Or maybe because Bryson knew her so well, he sensed her current unease.

"I'm fine," she said, knowing she was lying, or at least fibbing. She was glad to see that, once they got inside, Andrea was talking to a woman near the doorway, apparently one of the dog owners since a nice, calm German shepherd was leashed at her side.

The dog and Lorrie traded nose sniffs, even as Harper/Hanna scanned the rest of the room. Nothing unusual there, just staff sitting on the floor or standing near other dogs, playing with them and giving them attention.

A strange thought rushed to Harper's mind. Did she know the woman who'd left for some reason other than her being a customer here?

There was something about her that brought Macie Smithston to mind, but that was ridiculous. For one thing, in addition to their recent communications, Harper had been in touch with Macie a lot over the past few years, both by email and phone, but they'd only seen each other in person occasionally. Harper remembered her as having moderate-length dark hair probably not long enough to be pulled into a ponytail that way. And this lady, along with her hat and boots, had been wearing a long-sleeved T-shirt and blue jeans, not nearly as dressy as she'd seen professional editor Macie look…but, of course, they weren't near the magazine offices here.

And why would Macie come here, if any of her editors did—which seemed highly unlikely? Betsy Bordley made more sense, since the article about Barky Boulevard had been published in her most recent *Pets and Love* magazine.

Harper wanted to slough off her ridiculous thoughts, but for the moment she approached Andrea, whose graying hair was loose around her face. "Looks like you've got a good crowd here today," she told Bryson's aunt, knowing he was right behind her. "We just saw another lady leave here as we were coming in. Which one is her dog?" Harper realized it might sound odd for her to even ask, but what the heck? And she continued to recall she was Hanna here, but remained in her own mind, where she was Harper.

Andrea looked confused for a moment, but then her expression cleared a little. "Oh, I think you're referring to that nice lady who just popped in for a visit a little while ago. She said she had heard about Barky Boulevard in that magazine article and wanted to see for herself what we were about. She looked around for a while, talked to some of our people and petted a few dogs, then thanked me and left."

Harper felt Bryson's harsh stare but just asked, "What did she talk about?"

"Oh, she just wanted more information about the

place and to see the employees who'd been mentioned without being identified and if everyone was here today."

Like her, Harper wondered, the visiting helper who happened to write that article about the place?

Or was she just overthinking this too, like she did so many other things these days? After all, she'd already figured that Macie was the least likely of her editors to show up here.

Wasn't she?

Harper had an urge to run outside and look for the woman, just to check her out. But enough time had passed that the woman most likely wasn't anywhere around here now.

She told herself to shrug it off.

She also told herself to let Bryson know, when they were alone, what a ridiculous thought she'd had.

And even if it was Macie, so what? Maybe she'd just enjoyed Harper's article and wanted to see the source of the story herself for some reason. Or research another one herself for her magazine. Ridiculous? Yes, but who knew?

Besides, if it had been her, why would she have dressed that way? Plus, she would have recognized Harper and said something.

Anyway, for now, Harper would just dig back down into her life here and spend some time in Barky Boulevard, and become Hanna for a while. And when she could get back on her computer she would send a friendly email to Macie following up on their earlier exchange and not mention her silly assumption, and see Macie's reaction.

But before she could get into her work of sorts here, Bryson said softly, "Hey, let's go into my office for a minute."

When she looked into his eyes, she saw something inquisitive and figured he'd want to know what she'd just been thinking about. Of course, she would tell him.

Which she did, as they sat down at his desk and she bent over to pat Lorrie.

"So what was going on about that lady we saw here?" Bryson asked. "You seemed to want a lot of info from Andrea."

Harper just shrugged and made herself laugh a little. "I'm just letting my imagination run wild about everything these days. The woman resembled one of my editors, but it definitely wasn't her. Your aunt's answers to my questions made that clear."

"Did they?" he asked sharply. "Which of your editors? And when were you last in contact with her?"

Harper told him. "But Macie urged me to visit her offices in San Diego as soon as possible. It doesn't make sense that she wouldn't be there now."

Or did it? Macie always seemed to want things her way, and Harper wasn't fully cooperating. Still, why show up here, especially since Harper had made it clear in her article that she'd researched the place a while ago and was no longer around?

No, that couldn't have been her. But Harper told herself again to contact Macie soon and see if she could subtly learn if that editor was at home.

"Got it," Bryson said, leaning toward Harper and taking her hand that wasn't petting Lorrie. He also looked into her eyes. "But I'll do a little follow-up just to make sure you're right."

And for some reason, that calmed Harper…a lot.

* * *

Okay, so what was that really about? Bryson wondered as he left his office with Harper a few minutes later so they could work with the dogs and people here before heading back to the shelter.

Like Harper, and also his aunt and others, he sat down on the floor and began to play with one of the closest dogs, a black standard poodle who was clearly enamored with playing tug-of-war with a long, woven dog toy. Good. Bryson could play without thinking too hard about what he was doing, just what he really wanted to think about.

"Grrr, Manfred," he called to the dog as he pulled at the toy and continued to think.

He knew Harper well enough to trust her gut instincts, as she generally did, he believed, and that woman had clearly reminded her of her editor in San Diego she'd been communicating with recently.

And his own gut instincts? He trusted them too, even more. He could just let this go, sure, but he knew he'd be stewing over whether Harper had been right, as she probably would be, until he could make sure she'd been wrong. Or not.

Heck, he wanted to check on this Macie, one way or another. He might be on leave now but was still in law enforcement. Plus, he had a good contact in Scott, who was a local undercover cop.

One way or another, he could contact the San Diego PD and ask them to covertly check on whether she was home, or whether she could have visited Chance.

But what if it was her? So what? Barky Boulevard was featured in Harper's article as they agreed, and the fact that Harper had been in town a while back was evident. Why would that editor come here now? She wouldn't assume Harper was still here, would she? And even if she did, she was at least Harper's business associate and maybe a friend, not a threat.

Or was she?

Chapter 19

Harper, as Hanna, kept playing with Lorrie and the other dogs, which she enjoyed as usual, but that wasn't what she concentrated on.

She kept glancing at Bryson, who did the same thing while sitting near his aunt on the floor.

For now, she should just wait and let Bryson do his law-enforcement thing and check on Macie's whereabouts before trying to contact the editor. That would be most appropriate, right?

But even though she recognized the ridiculousness of the possibility, her mind kept focusing on whom she'd thought she'd seen.

If it was Macie, why was she here? Just for research on her own, possibly for an article in her magazine?

More likely, she was looking for Harper, or at least where she'd been. But again, why?

To check more on those threats and be there when the harasser did whatever to Harper? Or might it be totally innocent research, again assuming Harper hadn't gone even more nuts for considering Macie?

Still, she really wanted to talk to her. And when they got a break a short while later when one of the owners came in to pick up a pup and Andrea stood to greet him, Harper rose too, and saw that Bryson did as well.

"Have you contacted anyone about confirming Macie is in her San Diego office?" she asked, keeping her voice low as she got as close to Bryson as she thought might be appropriate here in public.

"I made a few calls before," he said, "but no response yet."

"Calls," Harper repeated. "That's what I'd like to do. Call her, to see what she says. And couldn't the cops then check her GPS to see if she's in the area?"

"Yeah," he said. "And she could then check your GPS to find you too."

"Well, if that was her, she already knows where I am." Harper sighed. "Okay, I get it. I won't call her, at least not now. But how about if I do my normal thing and send her an email?"

"Go for it," Bryson responded, nodding toward his office. He clearly wasn't going to join her at the moment, which was fine. She could handle this.

And determine if she'd continue to obey him and not make that call.

She took Lorrie outside briefly without asking Bryson to accompany them, and watched people in their environment.

No sign of that lady, whoever she was.

Harper got another idea. When she finally returned inside and sat down at Bryson's desk on her computer, she drafted an email to Macie, and to Sally, the publisher. Just wanted to let you know I'm trying to work out a visit to your offices in the next week or so, she wrote, lying. Are you both there?

She spent some more time checking her emails, as well as social media to see if there were any more references to her recent stories. And there were a couple, fortunately good ones about Barky doggy day care, as well as what a wonderful thing Dr. Jantis was doing.

Another day of good stuff that made Harper think maybe she could leave here and visit San Diego, or at least go home.

And she almost immediately got a return email from Macie, who sounded delighted that Harper might visit them, indicating she was at their offices now. She copied Sally, as usual. And soon Sally joined in their email conversation, saying she would be happy to see Harper and didn't deny that Macie was around, either.

Harper had to rethink things. Why did that woman remind her of Macie? She didn't look much like her, and she hadn't said anything to indicate she might have recognized Harper too.

And, again, why would she be here anyway?

Harper spent another minute on her computer, then looked down at Lorrie, who sat up and began wagging her butt.

"My imagination could just be at work again," Harper told her pup. Still, if whoever Harper saw did happen to be one of her editors, that woman had appeared to wear a kind of disguise. She'd seen Betsy a few times in person, as well as online. Betsy also had darkish hair, though it was even shorter than Macie's. She was older than Macie and had some wrinkles on her face, but Harper hadn't been close enough to make out many facial features of the visitor, let alone wrinkles. But the hat, the

sunglasses, the possibly false ponytail, the tall boots…
Who knew?

Still, the email she sent to Betsy was just general
and nice and asked if she had any particular ideas for
further articles from Harper, who also said she was researching some possibilities. Oh, and was Betsy interested in visiting the subject of this most recent article,
or had she? *Pets and Love* was headquartered in Sac-
ramento, which was still a distance from Chance, but
closer than San Diego.

Harper spent a few more minutes on the computer,
after she'd gotten back on it, this time checking her
social-media accounts, and even posting a few comments at some places where her recent articles were
mentioned, mostly on the magazines' Facebook and X/
Twitter pages. She was essentially just checking in, letting the world, besides her editors, know she was still
around and interested in what people had to say about
her stories, especially if they weren't panning them.

And looking yet again for any threats. Who'd sent
them?

Why had they stopped?

And why had Harper let them take over her life this way?

Sure, she had a vivid imagination. That was why she
was good at what she did: writing.

The threats hadn't been her imagination, of course,
but there'd been no recent follow-up, which was a good
thing.

But maybe that indicated she'd taken them too seri-
ously.

Maybe she should never have tried to run away and
become a staff member at the Chance Animal Shelter.

It would have been a shame if she hadn't met up with Bryson again, but she wouldn't have known that possibility if she hadn't panicked and tried to find a way to hide from whoever was possibly just trying to play a joke on her—a not particularly funny joke.

"Enough," she finally said aloud to Lorrie, who stood up and looked at her expectantly, waiting to see what they were doing next.

Time to go back out and pretend to be an employee here at Barky Boulevard.

When they returned to the play area, it was crowded, as usual. But Bryson wasn't there.

Harper/Hanna's mind started jutting in multiple directions. Was he out working with local law enforcement? Trying to find that mysterious woman on his own?

Or just doing his usual thing of helping Scott at the shelter?

Well, she figured he would show up eventually.

And he did, a short while later. He joined Andrea and her and the others, playing with the visiting dogs, but not for long.

He soon said to Hanna, "I think it's time for us to leave."

He didn't mention where they'd go, but the expression on his handsome but serious face suggested that answer.

Back to the Chance Animal Shelter.

Bryson soon had Harper in the car with him, driving them both to the shelter. Today, he sort of wondered about the state of Harper's mind.

Yes, he'd seen that woman leave Barky too, and had no idea who she was. Andrea had indicated she had dropped in just to see what the place was like. Maybe she had read Harper's article and was curious.

As Bryson had thought earlier, he trusted Harper though, and her instincts, so he had put out a few feelers to try to identify the woman. Sherm and Kara had both been available when he'd called, and they indicated they'd have their patrol officers keep an eye out for her, although it might be difficult to identify her from her description and without knowing if she was driving a car in the area. Sherm also said he'd check with the police department in San Diego to see if he could get them to do a quick visit to the magazine offices there to learn if all the editors and staff were present.

But who knew if they'd do it, and how long it might take?

And Bryson still couldn't help wondering, despite how much he cared for Harper and was concerned about her, if doing all this, based on her odd and quick impression of the Barky visitor, was worth anyone else's trouble.

"You okay back there, Lorrie?" Harper leaned over the back seat slightly and checked on her dog. Her love for her pup was just another reason Bryson cared for her so much.

But there were a lot of other reasons too, so, yes, he would do all he could to relieve her concerns about that woman, despite having no reason so far to understand them. After all, even if she turned out to be the editor Harper suspected, so what?

Although… Well, yes, Bryson would have some concerns too, if that was the case. He'd want to know the reason for her coming here as well.

To locate Harper? Unlikely, since the article hadn't been published in her magazine, and it had been clear it had been researched a while back…although that was a lie. But who else would know that?

"So how is she doing?" he responded to Harper's question to Lorrie, who was unlikely to bark back.

"She looks good, as usual." Harper had turned back around and was smiling at Bryson, which made him feel good as well.

"Glad to hear it. We're almost at the shelter."

He checked the traffic around them, as he always did when getting near Chance Animal Shelter. Not many other cars were on the street. Unlikely that anyone would be paying attention to them or where they were heading, but being careful like that was one of the things Scott generally hammered into the heads of those, like Bryson, who weren't local cops, but could come into and out of the place.

Sure, people could bring in animals needing new homes, but the website made it clear they needed to call first and schedule an appointment. And no one who just showed up there could just come in, bringing an animal or not.

More because of the human staff members than the animals, of course. No sense jeopardizing their protection.

Bryson prepared to call Scott to get him to have Nella or someone else appropriate let them in shortly, after they'd parked in the usual outside lot.

But before he did, as he began to slow down, he noticed another car, an older silver sedan, also slowing down behind them.

Interesting. Just being careful in the small amount of traffic?

Or was the driver watching them?

Probably not, but just in case, Bryson sped up. So did that car, remaining behind them but not close enough for him to read the license plate in his rearview mirror.

Okay, in case it was something he really did need to be wary of, he headed back in the direction of Barky Boulevard, leaving the shelter area.

"What's going on?" Harper had noticed what he was doing.

"Just being extra cautious. There was a car behind us that could have been following us, or not. I decided to make it appear we were heading elsewhere, just in case."

"Who would be following us?" Harper asked, sounding nervous.

"Oh, your strange lady friend, of course." Bryson laughed, hoping he sounded funny. "Or not. But you know me. I've got protecting you on my mind, so even if I don't have all the answers, if I have questions I'll try to figure them out."

"Got it." Harper seemed to attempt to laugh back, although her voice was hoarse.

For now, Bryson just drove by Barky Boulevard, but didn't stop there either. Instead, he drove by the Chance police station after calling Kara. "Probably nothing," he told her, but he described what had just happened.

A cop car came up behind them in just a minute, and Bryson drove around Chance's downtown, past Barky Boulevard once more, talking now and then on his car phone system to Kara.

No, there was no indication of the car he described

anywhere around them. But Kara unsurprisingly pointed out there were quite a few other silver sedans in downtown Chance, though not near their area.

Bryson soon felt comfortable enough for them to head back to the shelter and park in the usual, nearly empty lot in the shadows at the rear. He'd already called to let Nella know their arrival time, and they quickly exited the car with Lorrie, not letting her sniff around this time, and Bryson was happy when Nella soon let them into the usual door, which she again locked behind them.

"Everything okay?" asked the pretty, brown-eyed woman wearing her usual blue Chance Animal Shelter T-shirt. She looked concerned, as if she sensed their unease.

"Sure." Bryson hoped he sounded sincere even though that was a bit of a lie. He remained a little concerned despite the situation having seemingly amounted to nothing.

"Hope so," added Harper, bending to stroke Lorrie's head.

At least they were inside the tall shelter walls. And Bryson would make sure to meet briefly with Scott that night, maybe at dinnertime, and let him know what was going on: Harper's concern about that stranger, plus the small incident regarding that slowing car.

And here, Harper would continue to be safe.

Chapter 20

Okay, Harper thought as she changed the water in Lorrie's bowl in her apartment's kitchen and started getting her pup's breakfast ready—the premium canned food Harper liked best for her plus a little kibble, as always. Fortunately, this shelter provided many kinds of foods for its animal residents, and these were among them.

Two days had passed since she'd last left the Chance Animal Shelter and done a stint at Barky Boulevard. Two days since she'd seen that woman who'd somehow made her mind race, and her imagination too. The stranger who might not have been anyone Harper had ever seen before. Or she might have been someone Harper knew, who was important in her life.

Really?

She had started to focus more on that oddity than anything else, including her research and writing.

And even her fear of more threats, although if any came in, that could change in an instant.

She thought she might be letting the stress she felt overwhelm her and had started making notes on her computer about various ways of handling unanticipated stress.

Maybe someday she could write an article about that too, although it wouldn't be as fun to write as her animal stories.

And would she ever want to admit any of this to the world? Online anonymous threats leading to a writer's changing her entire life and not being sure she did the right thing. And then seeing people she thought she recognized or not, maybe just an offshoot of all that stress. But—

"Hey, you ready to go down to breakfast?" Bryson asked. He'd just taken his shower, after she had hers, and when she looked around and saw him in the kitchen doorway he looked as handsome as ever in his short-sleeved blue T-shirt and jeans.

No, he wasn't any more dressed up than she was, also in jeans but with a peach-colored T-shirt that had the shelter name emblazoned on it.

"Sure," she replied. "As soon as Lorrie finishes her breakfast."

"That's fine. Looks like she's really concentrating on it and should be done soon."

"You got it," Harper said. "That's my dedicated pup." She took a few steps closer to Bryson while they waited. That felt right.

They'd been close all night, after all, which had become a new and resurrected habit.

But today, as far as she knew, Bryson would be going out into the world again to Barky Boulevard, without her, as he had yesterday.

She remained here. She remained under protection.

She remained frustrated about not having gone back to her real life yet.

And she remained frustrated that her staying here wasn't only because Scott, and Bryson, kept telling her this was best. No, it was also because she remained too afraid to be out in the world after those unsolved threats despite their waning somewhat.

Which also made her angry with herself.

Not that she'd let them know.

In a few minutes, Lorrie had finished licking the dregs from her bowl. "Ready to go see your doggy friends?" Harper asked the pup, knowing she was about to become Mia again during the time they were around other people at the shelter. After all this time, she had become used to it, and was glad, and amused, that Bryson had too. Like her, he had to keep track of their current location and therefore who she was, which changed a lot. But they'd both done well, fortunately.

"I gather she's ready," Bryson said now. He retrieved Lorrie's leash from the edge of the kitchen counter. Harper rarely brought anything downstairs with her. Certainly not her phone, or even anything to make notes, which always seemed strange to the writer in her. But that was the way things were these days. And maybe for a long time to come.

Soon, they walked down the steps of the apartment building, heading for the cafeteria as they always did at this hour. And they weren't the only ones. By now, Mia recognized, and said good morning to, nearly everyone, all also wearing Chance Animal Shelter T-shirts though in different colors, including Kathy, Chessie and Leonard, and also Bibi, whom Mia had only recently met and who had a gap between her front teeth. There were other staffers around too. Mia was the only one with a dog with her, since she was the only one at the shelter who'd brought her own dog along.

She didn't see Scott or Nella on the stairs, though they'd undoubtedly join the group in the cafeteria.

They entered the main cafeteria room, already full of staffers there for breakfast. Mia noticed Sara was at the serving table, as the cook often was.

"Let's all eat breakfast together," Bibi said, and she seemed to scan the cafeteria for a table where there'd be room for all of them who'd just entered.

Mia noticed a couple of empty seats at the main table where Nella already was and assumed Scott would be joining her.

Mia would prefer being with them and considered a gentle way to refuse Bibi's invitation. But Bryson was the one who said, "Sorry. Sounds good, but we already have places being saved for us."

Which was probably true, since they did sit with Scott and Nella most of the time, but Mia was glad Bryson had told Bibi.

They all headed to the serving table, Lorrie as always at Mia's side, and dished out helpings of scrambled eggs and fried potatoes and other usual fare. Mia got a cup of coffee, then followed Bryson, who'd also chosen his breakfast, to their expected seats.

Sure enough, Scott and Nella had saved places for them.

They all started eating and talking and discussing the probable training sessions with the shelter dogs that they'd get to do that day.

Except that, when things slowed down at the serving table and pretty much everyone was seated, Scott stood up. "I have an announcement to make," he said, then walked to the front of the room at the end of the long tables. "Excuse me, everyone," he called out, and everyone became quiet to listen to him. "Just want to let you know that at around ten this morning we have a couple of families coming in to look at the rescue dogs we have here to hopefully adopt some, so you know what that means."

"We're tethered in our rooms till they leave," Leonard called. He'd also stood from farther down the table.

"Exactly. We don't want anyone to see any of you." Scott's tone made it sound as if he was calling the staffers with bad news, but Mia knew keeping them invisible here was for their protection.

"Okay, our noble leader," Leonard continued, "we'll obey you."

Which Mia certainly would. Bryson? Unlikely, since he'd probably leave for Barky Boulevard right after breakfast, though he hadn't invited Harper/Hanna that day.

Which was fine with her.

Right now, when she looked toward him, he just smiled wryly, obviously figuring what she was thinking.

Did she wish she was going with him today?

Well, hopefully soon again. But continuing to hang out here for the moment would work, especially since she intended to take some time out from the training, maybe earlier than ten o'clock, and go back to her apartment with Lorrie and do some work on her computer. As always.

It was only around eight thirty when they finished eating, so a while still remained before the staff members would need to stay in their rooms.

When Bryson left soon thereafter, Mia stayed in the shelter's central area after joining some of the other staffers inside the shelter buildings and bringing out some of the dogs to exercise and train.

Mia maintained Lorrie's leash, but her pup got along well with many of the others, so they soon were working with Ashy and Leonard. Mia really enjoyed it, and Lorrie seemed to as well.

But after about an hour, Mia decided it was time to follow her real plans of the day. After another short session of getting both dogs to sit, stay, then heel, while watching some of the other pups in the central area obey similar commands by other staff members, Mia stood off to one side and made herself appear worn out.

"I think Lorrie and I need an early break," she told Leonard. The young guy's Chance Animal Shelter T-shirt was charcoal-gray, and he grinned as he looked at her.

"What, you're tired of playing with the dogs? Or are you just tired of playing with me?"

Mia laughed. "I'll let you figure that out. Meantime, I'll hopefully see you at lunchtime, once we can leave our apartments again, and maybe we can do some more training together this afternoon."

"Sure. Maybe."

Mia figured that was his acceptance of her leaving. She glanced around the area and didn't see Scott or Nella with the large group of staff members and dogs, and figured they were inside.

They wouldn't mind her leaving early. They knew what she'd be up to, but Scott had hopefully come to trust her since she'd run her prior articles by him, as promised.

What would she work on today? Well, she had some new ideas about stories to research, maybe one or more of the centers that took in injured or abandoned newborn wildlife to care for until they could be taken to an appropriate location and released.

Researching those places in person was always delightful and intriguing, but for now she'd just get in touch with some of her contacts to interview, or get introductions to others in the same field, from afar.

"Lorrie, come," she told her pup, pulling gently on the leash attached to her harness. With a wiggle in her walk, Lorrie accompanied Mia to the apartment building, where they took the elevator so Lorrie wouldn't have to struggle with the stairs this time.

Mia used her key card to let them into their small unit. She shut the door behind them and sighed.

She missed the other person, Bryson, who shared this place with them. Well, he'd probably return around dinnertime, as he'd been doing.

In the meantime, she was safe here locked this deep into the shelter even without Bryson's direct protection.

"Okay, girl," Mia—now Harper again—said to her pup. "Let's make sure you have enough water." Which she did.

She got herself a drink of water too, and added ice to it from the freezer. Then she brought out her computer from its case and set it up on the kitchen table.

She took a deep breath before logging on and getting into her emails. It had been quite a while since she had received any threats, so she didn't expect any now.

Still—

Everything appeared fine initially. She started at the top of the list, and opened a new email from Macie, who'd copied Sally, as usual these days. Was she going to say anything about seeing Harper here? Not hardly. But she did ask, as a follow-up, when Harper would finally be visiting them in San Diego.

Harper considered what to say, then wrote back, I'm still working on plans. I'll let you know how they progress. That was noncommittal enough, she figured, but still somewhat positive.

After taking a sip of water and checking on Lorrie, who was lying on the floor beside her, she skimmed through more emails, some spam and a few from readers, which she enjoyed. No bad reviews or nasty remarks for the moment, at least.

Then there were emails from her other main editors, Wanda Grey and Betsy Bordley. They were each friendly yet a bit demanding, asking when they'd next get articles from Harper. Wanda even said she had an idea to run by Harper, who figured she'd respond soon.

But first, she noticed another, slightly older email from Macie. Of course, she had to open that one too, and she noticed right away that Sally hadn't been copied on it.

And then she gasped as she read it, clutching at her throat as her eyes teared up.

It said:

Okay, Harper—or Hanna, isn't it, there? I know you might have recognized me as I left Barky Boulevard after trying to track you down there and at the other locations that were sites of your recent stories. And there you were. Just so you know, I followed you again from a distance, including in my car when that guy drove you away from the doggy day care place, and my research indicated that guy, who owns the day care facility, is your former boyfriend. I saw you near that Chance Animal Shelter and figured you were going there to do a story on it, and once I drove away after you or your guy apparently noticed me I did some of my own research in town and learned what that shelter is really about. I don't have much information on it yet, but enough. And I gathered as I continued to watch the place from a distance that you might be staying there for protection or whatever, and that might be why I haven't seen an article by you about it. So here's what I want: I've been going back and forth to my office, and now I want you to accompany me there right away and settle down to write only for Puppies, Kittens and Humans. If you don't, I'll publish something about the rumors on what Chance Animal Shelter is really about. I figure you'll want to protect it, so come along with me. Get back to me soon. Real soon. Oh, and by the way. Those threats you received that apparently made you run away? Guess who sent them. Me! So you'd better listen to me or some of them will come true fast. And if you tell anyone about this, the world will learn about that shelter right away.

Harper was crying. Why was Macie doing this? And what was Harper going to do? Not listening to Macie would mean a lot of people here at the shelter would be in greater danger, soon.

But if she did as Macie said, how could she, let alone her career, possibly survive?

Bryson was on his way back to the Chance Animal Shelter from Barky Boulevard fast. A lot earlier than usual when he didn't have Harper along. But something seemed strange when he tried to contact Scott with a question, and he needed to know what was going on.

And it definitely was strange. When Nella met him at the gate and let him in, she looked highly stressed. There were tears in her brown eyes, and her T-shirt just hung from her sagging shoulders.

He was about to ask what was wrong when she began, "Have you talked to Mia, Bryson? There's clearly something wrong but she's not telling us, except that she's packed up and told us she wants to leave the shelter right away and has asked us to let her out. I think she was hoping she'd get away before you came back, if you did today. But—"

"Where is she?" he demanded.

"In Scott's office, trying to convince him to open one of the exits. They're still talking, I think."

"I'll join them," Bryson said.

He immediately rushed past Nella and hurried up to Scott's office, where he heard raised voices through the closed door. He didn't even wait to knock before bursting in.

Harper stood in front of Scott's desk, leaning toward him. Both recognized Bryson's presence and turned toward him.

"Glad you're here," Scott said at once, also standing, his arms folded over his chest. "You need to talk some sense into Harper, or at least get her to tell us what's happening, why she suddenly wants to leave the shelter right now, where she wants to go and anything else relevant. She worked so hard to convince me to let her to stay here, and now—"

"Now I need to leave." Harper glared from Scott to Bryson. Her lower lip was sticking out, her eyebrows furrowed as if she was furious.

But there were the tears in her eyes. And the way Lorrie pawed at her legs made it clear the dog sensed her emotion and was trying to help.

Bryson knew Scott well enough to figure that the shelter director and undercover cop would have been cool and calm earlier, trying to get Harper's motivation from her. And he knew Harper well enough to understand she had to have a good reason for this.

"Let's all sit down and talk about this," Bryson said, trying to keep his cool. "And I agree with you, Scott, not to open any of the shelter exits to let Harper leave until we're all in agreement."

Which he knew he most likely would never be, not unless Harper gave a convincing explanation.

And he figured her reason had to be because of those threats somehow.

Had the menacing person found her?

Were there more threats? And for her to act this way, he concluded something major worried her.

Which meant she wasn't the only one likely to be in danger.

She sat looking down at Lorrie, not meeting his eyes or Scott's. Bryson asked immediately, "So who's in danger now besides you?"

She looked up at him, understanding and anger visible in her lovely green eyes. "How did you know?" She held up her hand. "No, don't bother answering. You're just guessing."

"And I suspect it's a good guess, based on what I know about you and how you're reacting."

She sighed and bit her lower lip. "Yeah," she said softly. "It is a good guess. But I was told things would get even worse if I told anyone about it."

"Well, don't write it in an article," Bryson said, "but I think it's time you let Scott and me know. And you can feel assured that these two cops will do all we can to make sure things are okay."

Harper's expression changed, almost to one of relief. And her expression, as she looked at him, also appeared grateful. And caring. And made him want to take her into his arms.

But he just waited.

And the story she told him didn't surprise him at all.

Chapter 21

Okay. Taking a deep breath, Harper told them both about that email from Macie. Then, at their request, she showed it to them, handing Bryson her phone first.

"But I don't understand why she's doing this," she said. "Why she wants me to go to the magazine's office at all, let alone now. I work remotely as a freelancer, and she knows it and has seemed okay with buying articles from me before…until recently, at least. But I guess she didn't really like them after all. Wanted me to stop, or at least stop submitting to her magazine. But why didn't she just tell me? Why threaten me?"

"That's what we need to find out," Scott said.

"What we *will* find out," Bryson growled.

"But, please, don't do anything to indicate I told you about it," Harper pleaded. "I know you'll both do everything possible to make sure the Chance Animal Shelter's real purpose stays secret, but I believe that threat above all others of Macie's. If she finds out I told anyone about her admissions and demand to go with her, she'll tell the world everything by writing articles in her magazine and even more—online, on social media, and whatever."

"Oh, I believe she will try," Scott agreed. "But we won't let her."

"But how—"

"We'll figure it out." Bryson, who'd been sitting beside her, across from Scott at his desk, reached over and took her hand. "And don't worry about this. None of it is your fault."

Harper felt her eyes tear up even more. Oh, yes, that was one of the major things she had been concerned about. She didn't want word to get out there. And she definitely didn't want to be responsible for it if Macie disclosed everything, which she would be if her revealing what Macie had told her was the reason the editor decided to blab.

But Bryson's hand on hers, squeezing gently, did make her feel a little better. Cared for, at least.

Excused? Well, she wouldn't excuse herself.

"So what are we going to do?" Scott asked.

"I have an idea," Bryson said. "But we're going to have to be damned careful if we follow through with it. It'll involve more danger to Harper."

"That's okay with me," she replied right away, "if we can finally work things out, deal with Macie, and get this over with."

And so they pondered it aloud, the three of them. Harper felt uncomfortable when the men helped her draft an email response to Macie. After all, she was the writer, not them. But they knew best, hopefully, about how to deal with making certain this wonderful shelter survived and wasn't harmed by letting people, including those who'd initially endangered each of the residents, know what it really was about: helping not only pets in need, but also humans who needed a place to stay for their protection,

A short while later, after they were through drafting and discussing, she pressed Send, and the email was gone. No turning back.

And she wasn't surprised when a response from Macie came quickly:

Yes, I'm in Chance right now. I've got my car. Glad you're being smart. I'll drive us to San Diego. I assume you can get out of that shelter with those damn high fences. Meet me at the parking lot at the far side of the park across the street at one o'clock. You'll get out of that shelter by then, right? Oh, and just so you know, I have an article ready to publish in Puppies, Kittens and Humans right away, just by pushing a button on my phone, if it turns out you've disclosed this or done anything else wrong or if anyone follows us. It's okay to bring your dog. You won't be going back.

Harper took a deep breath and showed the email to the men, to Bryson first. "I need to be there," she said.

"Yeah, you do," Scott responded. Harper saw him stare at Bryson, as if challenging him to disagree, but he didn't.

"Fine with me," he said. "But don't count on not being followed, although not obviously. You'll have your phone, so your GPS will help. But we need to figure out what else to do to stop that madwoman, without you getting hurt."

Harper appreciated that and certainly hoped they figured out what to do. But she doubted anything would work.

And so, she would soon be with Macie. Under her control.

Maybe for the rest of her life, however short it might be.

"Okay, here's what we'll do. Let's call Sherm and Kara before you leave, Harper—like right now."

Scott talked the most when the police chief and his assistant were on the phone. They already knew about Harper's general situation, but he explained this latest, and greatest, threat, both to the shelter and to her.

"We need to figure out a way to capture this lunatic editor," Scott said.

"Before she tries to send her article or whatever that will disclose everything about the Chance Animal Shelter," added Harper.

"Or do anything to hurt Harper." That was Bryson. He looked at her with care and concern. She wanted to hug him.

She also wanted to get out of there and deal with Macie, but knew she had to listen to all these cops to do her best to bring the situation to as satisfying a conclusion as possible.

"No police patrols or other vehicles following the subject car once Harper gets into it," Scott continued. "Can you have unmarked patrols that just sweep along the streets where they are and report in without looking too obvious?"

"You know we can," Kara said.

"We'll need to let you follow by using the GPS on Harper's phone," Bryson continued. "But once you're ready to bring Macie down, you'll have to use a cell-phone jammer to make sure she can't forward whatever communication she plans to send to get that damn disclosing article she's written published."

"I assume she'll be contacting the publisher of her

magazine to do that, so jamming any communication with her then sounds perfect," Harper added.

"Okay, then," Sherm said. "Give us the particulars. When and where are they meeting up?"

Harper told them the gist of Macie's communication, including the time and location she was supposed to show up to start her horrendous ride with the editor.

She understood why they needed to see the threat Macie just made about revealing all if Harper talked, so she forwarded a copy of that email to them as potential evidence if they arrested Macie.

And Sherm and Kara said they'd dive right into it.

Which was a good thing, since it was already after twelve o'clock.

And so Harper and Lorrie went to her small apartment, accompanied by Bryson, and put most of her belongings into her suitcase and backpacks, including things for her dog. They returned downstairs, where Scott led them cautiously to the gate and let them out, hopefully not seen by any staffers. Harper was glad when Bryson gave her a quick goodbye kiss. And wondered if she would see him again.

Oh, yes. She had to.

As long as she remained alive.

There she was then, outside. Harper carefully led Lorrie across the street and into the park, over to its far side, where the parking area was.

Sure enough, Macie stood there by a fairly new, clearly expensive silver sedan. She was the same height, and her dark hair the same moderate length as Harper recalled. She was middle-aged, with a few lines on her round face.

Not the same as the woman Harper had recently seen who reminded her of Macie, but close enough.

And now she grinned as she saw Harper. "Hey, passenger," she said as Harper drew close. "Let's get going." She took Harper's bags and put them in the trunk after opening the back door so Lorrie could get inside.

She motioned for Harper to get into the passenger seat, which she did, and fastened the seat belt, but she wondered how things would be on this journey.

Safe for all of them, she hoped, but with Macie taken into police custody somewhere along the line, before she could do anything to harm the shelter and its occupants. Or Harper.

"Okay, we're on our way," Macie said triumphantly. "San Diego, here we come." She pushed a button to start the car, and they were off.

"Okay," Harper said after a minute. "I'd really appreciate it if you'd tell me what's going on, why you threatened me so much before about my writing and otherwise, and why you're doing this, dragging me to your magazine office. What are you going to do with me there?"

They'd stopped at a light, and Macie glared at her with furious hazel eyes. "Oh, you should know why, honey. You've somehow achieved the kind of writing career I always wanted but haven't yet achieved myself. And it drives me bananas that Sally keeps asking for more articles from you and has even hinted she'd love to hire you as another senior editor, maybe even senior to me. Sure, you write good stuff, but mine's a lot better, though it doesn't always get published. I sure as hell don't want a petty freelancer like you to upend my current career, such as it is."

"I'm sorry you feel that way," Harper said, unsure how to react but determined to have a conversation with Macie that would lead to better answers. "I didn't want to harm you or your career, just keep my own going. But you—you indicated in some of those threats that you might even kill me, and that just doesn't seem a logical reason."

"I threatened you to try to get you to quit," Macie said through clenched teeth, "but that didn't happen. I stopped sending threats, by the way, when I thought that would cause you to finally return to your usual location but that didn't do it, so I had to think of what else to do, which I did. And now, like it or not, you're going to join me as an editor for *Puppies, Kittens and Humans* and I'll get to show Sally how much better I am, both at writing and editing. Fortunately, she hasn't paid much attention recently to when I'm in the office, so I've been able to go back and forth often without her knowing I'm gone. Anyway, once we've shown her the truth she can boot you back to the rest of your life while my own life is lifted to where it should be, as the only, and her favorite, editor and writer."

Really? That sounded rather insane. In fact, it was clear that Macie had major mental issues.

But could she be stopped before she wrecked Harper's professional life that way, and, even more important, the lives of the Chance Animal Shelter staff members?

"Oh, and in case you're wondering, honey, I'm keeping close watch on our surroundings. Did you tell anyone what was going on?" Harper opened her mouth to claim she had listened, that she hadn't told anyone anything, but Macie continued, "Don't bother answering. If you say no, I won't believe you anyway. And I'm ready to send that article about the shelter to Sally with a push of my finger, right here, if I get any notion that you ignored what I said and blabbed. It'll come with an introductory note about how important it is to get the story up at least on social media right away, even before publishing it in print." She took her left hand off the steering wheel and reached into a small shelf on the car door, then pulled out a cell phone, which she kept in her hand, with a finger near what Harper figured was the send button for that scary email.

Where are you, cops? Harper's mind raced, but she didn't dare look around them. *And where are you, Bryson?* Was he finding a way to join the authorities as they did what they'd discussed with Sherm and Kara? She wasn't thrilled that her mind cried out for him that way, as if she relied on him for all her safety, but she did.

She wished she'd programmed her own phone so he, and the others, could hear her conversation with Macie, but they'd discussed that and determined it was too dangerous. Find her via her GPS? That should work and not be too obvious. But having a phone call open seemed illogical.

She did look through the windshield and see them negotiating streets, some she recognized, but others she didn't. She assumed they were heading for a highway, though, to start taking them south from Chance to San Diego.

How far did the jurisdiction of the Chance Police Department go?

Would they stop Macie soon enough?

Harper could only wish as she glanced, hopefully not

obviously, toward the cars of various types and sizes around them. No marked police vehicles, though that wasn't surprising.

But were the authorities nearby yet, ready to stop Macie soon?

Bryson drove the car that had Sherm in it. Not Bryson's own SUV, which Macie might have seen with Harper in it and therefore recognized, but an older, somewhat dinged-up gray sedan that shouldn't be an attention-getter.

They spoke with cops in other nearby unmarked cars on official radios, though. None of their vehicles remained in the field of vision of Macie's car, but drove behind it or passed in front of it on cross streets.

Keeping watch on it until they reached an area where they could all veer closer and get Macie stopped.

He could only hope they'd be able to surround that car soon, in the right place to shut it down as safely as possible. That was everyone's goal here, so he didn't say anything.

He just drove.

Sherm was beside him, in the passenger seat, and he checked their coordinates often on the GPS screen on his phone. No such screen on the dashboard of this old car.

The police chief also spoke a lot on the radio, and Bryson could hear the conversations about the intersections being passed. And more intersections.

Until— "This could work," a male voice said over the radio, mentioning Chance Avenue and Forest Street. "Not much traffic here, in fact none I see at the moment. And we've got vehicles all around that can center in and surround that car, get it stopped with no streets or other turnoffs around. Plus, there's a copter nearby that we'll have fly over at the same time. You wanted them to use a signal jammer too, right?"

"Right. Let's do it," Sherm said, then aimed a glance at Bryson. "You heard?"

"Sure did. They're a block in front of us now, right?"

"Right, and there are other vehicles of ours between us and them and all around them. We're going in."

"And that copter's jammer will prevent any communication leaving that car, right—like an email telling someone to publish the potentially damaging article that woman mentioned?"

"Exactly."

Bryson hoped it worked. Really hoped. He'd been around here long enough to recognize how important it was to many lives that no one understand what the shelter was really about. How many of the staffers' enemies would leap on the place if they realized their potential victims were housed and under protection there.

He didn't want to find out, or have anyone else learn it either.

"Here we go," said the voice over the radio. At the same time, Bryson heard the sound of a helicopter. Good. Hopefully, the jamming of any signal from the car would take place but the police radios would continue to work.

At Sherm's direction, he drove forward faster, closer to Macie's car, and so did a couple other cars on the same road around them.

Then, he looked at cars pulling up from both sides of the upcoming intersection. He couldn't see any cars approaching on the same road coming the other way, but he assumed there were some too.

And in a very short time, they all came to a stop. Men and women jumped out of the various cars, mostly in plain clothes, but a few in uniform, weapons drawn.

They quickly approached Macie's car, as did Bryson. He wanted to get Harper out of there. Make sure she was okay.

Take her into his arms and—

He heard yelling, the breaking of at least one car window. Presumably, Macie wasn't just jumping out and cooperating.

But as he reached the car, the cops on the driver's side opened that door and aimed weapons at the person there, giving her orders to get out, and cooperate.

Which she did, cell phone in hand, pushing a button on it that hopefully wouldn't work.

Bryson, of course, headed for the passenger's side as that door opened too, and someone exited.

Harper.

He dashed to her, and she immediately saw him and hurried into his arms.

"Are you okay?" he demanded.

"I am now," she said.

Chapter 22

Two days had passed since the ordeal on the road with Macie. Harper was at the Chance Animal Shelter, in her apartment, finishing her packing. That felt familiar, since she'd brought nearly everything with her before, when she'd left with Macie. But she'd returned temporarily, and this would be her last time here to pack.

Since that day, she had given her official statement to a district attorney at the police station, where Macie had been placed, appropriately, in solitary confinement. Harper really wasn't familiar with criminal law. Would Macie be tried here for her crimes or someplace else?

Having it done in Chance seemed most fitting. Harper hoped that those indicting Macie wouldn't hesitate to charge her with various offenses, maybe including things like kidnapping and criminal threats and harassment, and hopefully a lot more, assuming a guilty verdict would mean Macie could remain in prison for a long, long time. By herself. With no one believing anything she said.

And then there was Harper's career. During a phone call the next day while she was alone in her apartment, Harper had reported to Sally Effling some of what had happened, since her senior editor wouldn't be returning home.

And Macie had been in contact with Sally too, though she hadn't said much, only that things in her life had taken a bad turn so she had to quit her editorial job. And Sally indicated she believed there'd been people listening in, though she hadn't known who.

"So sorry about all this," Harper had said.

"Me too," Sally told her. "I'd been considering offering you a new editor's position alongside Macie, but this wasn't how I intended to do it. Now, it would just be you. You'd be able to work remotely, if you want. And even write more freelance articles for other publications, if you have time."

Really? Well, Harper wanted to ponder it, not respond immediately.

"I've got some things going on right now. Please let me think about it. Okay?"

Fortunately, Sally had agreed.

It was late morning now. Harper had gone out onto the facility grounds earlier and worked with staffers and dogs there with Lorrie for the last time. She wasn't planning on staying for lunch.

Bryson should be here soon. He had hung out with her for the rest of the day of her ordeal and the nights since then, though he'd gone to Barky Boulevard during the days, including now. He was returning with her car, and she'd drive him to the pet-sitting site, where he'd left his car, when she departed the shelter today.

First though, she wanted to talk to Scott and Nella one last time, so she left her luggage at the apartment door, and Lorrie and she took an elevator downstairs,

then went into the office building and took another elevator up to Scott's office. He'd said he would meet with
her there, and so would Nella.

Sure enough, they were in his office, and both stood
when Harper and Lorrie came in.

"You all set?" Nella rushed over to take Harper's
hand, and bend to pat Lorrie on the head.

"Just waiting for my car to arrive," Harper replied. She
hesitated. "Any word on what's going on with Macie?"
She knew they had most likely been in touch with Sherm
and Kara, who remained Scott's bosses.

"So far, all looks okay for keeping her in custody and
her eventual prosecution," Scott said. "We can only hope
it works out well and she's not able to get word out about
what she thinks she knows about this shelter."

"*Thinks* makes sense," Nella said. "One of the things
the prosecuting attorneys indicated to me that they're
doing is to focus on her mental issues, so if she is able
to communicate with anyone they can make highly appropriate claims of her instability. A shelter for people
in trouble here? Ridiculous! Just a job and residence for
the previously homeless." Nella laughed, then shrugged.

A knock sounded on the office door, and when Scott
called, "Come in," Bryson entered.

"I figured I'd find you here," he told Harper. "Are
you ready to leave?"

"Just about." Harper was so glad to see him she nearly
rushed over to give him a hug. Instead, she turned back
to face Scott and Nella. "But before I go, I just want to
thank you both so much, for letting me stay here, protecting me and, as it turned out, potentially facing disclo-

sure to the world of this wonderful place's real purpose, thanks to me."

"You're very welcome," Scott said, also approaching her and smiling as he put his hand out for a shake. "And we don't blame you for what that sick woman threatened. Hopefully, we've stopped her, and worst case we'll discredit anything she says."

"I definitely hope so," Harper said. "And I'll send you an article about the animal portion of the shelter soon for your approval. If you okay it, I'll decide which of my favorite publications to submit it to, so it'll get published." *Puppies, Kittens and Humans*? It would depend on how she decided to respond to Sally. "That way the world will know about how wonderful an animal shelter this is, and that's all."

"Sounds great." Nella looked at her and smiled.

"I'll look forward to reading it," Scott said, "and hopefully approving it. And also staying in touch so I can let you know how things progress with Macie's quiet prosecution here."

"Thank you so much for that too." Harper took Scott's hand again, and then Nella's, then hugged them. "Hopefully I'll see you both again under better circumstances."

"I hope so too," Scott said.

Then, Lorrie's leash in her hand, Harper looked into Bryson's eyes. "Time to leave," she said.

"Yes, it is," he agreed.

Harper wasn't sure whether she was glad they didn't see any staff members on the way to collect her belongings, then leave through the gate as Nella let them out and locked it behind them. But she didn't want to explain to any of them why she was leaving now…forever.

Soon, Bryson and she were on their way to Barky Boulevard, with Harper driving her car, with its temporary new license plate. But she didn't just want to drop Bryson off. "Is it okay if I come in and say goodbye to Andrea?" she asked.

"Of course," Bryson said.

And to you too, Harper thought. *Goodbye for now. Or forever?*

She felt her eyes tear up as they had so often these days. Surely, they'd see each other again.

Especially because...well, with all that had happened again between Bryson and her, the way he'd taken care of her, the time they'd spent together lately... She couldn't deny it to herself any longer.

No matter what she had felt for Bryson before, she definitely was in love with him now.

But she was going home to pursue her career once more. He was staying here to help his aunt.

Oh, yes, they might not see each other again.

But could they at least keep in touch?

When they were together inside Barky Boulevard, before she left, she could at least ask him that.

And if they couldn't? If he didn't want to?

Well, she'd have to research and write a whole lot of articles about animals to keep her mind off him...and her heart from breaking.

They had reached the regular parking area for Barky Boulevard, and Bryson was glad when Harper parked her car beside his.

Sure, he'd go inside with her so she could say goodbye to his aunt. Only—

He had something to say first. Something to ask.

And so, before they got out of the car Bryson reached over and removed Harper's right hand from the steering wheel. He held it gently but firmly, as she looked at him with a quizzical expression.

"Is everything okay?" she asked.

"Only sort of."

"Then—"

But before she could ask any more, he leaned toward her and said, "I have an idea, Harper, and would like to talk to you. Can you just say hi to my aunt and other people there, then go into my office with me?"

"Sure." That quizzical expression grew more pronounced, and he wanted to kiss it away. Kiss *her*.

Not now though.

She got out of her car and so did he, and she removed Lorrie from the back seat, then gave her pup a chance to walk a little. Soon, they entered the noisy doggy day care center, which was definitely busy. Andrea was on the floor with her employees, working with some of the dogs.

"Hi," she called. "Want to join us?"

"Soon," Bryson responded. And he would want to get down and dirty with the dogs in a while if things didn't go well with Harper.

They went into his office then, Lorrie at Harper's feet as always, and Bryson closed the door behind them.

"What's up?" Harper asked. She remained a few feet away from him, but he closed the gap, standing in front of her. Time to risk everything, he thought. Right now.

"Harper, I know you're ready to get back to your real

life now that all the threats have stopped and the person who did that to you is in custody."

She nodded and just stood there, looking at him. "That's right. I—"

He didn't let her finish but grabbed her and pulled her into his arms. Her wonderful curves against him made him even more determined to do this. And to hope she would agree.

"I love you, Harper," he said, his lips against hers. "I have for a damn long time, and as I said, I have an idea."

He pulled back a little, and she looked straight into his eyes. "I love you too, Bryson. But—"

She did? She did! Oh, that felt good. But they still had things to work out. "Just listen for now. I know you can work remotely as a freelance journalist and dash off as needed to conduct your research. I'd like you to move in with me here, in Chance, for now. I've got some ideas about hiring a nearby financial advisor to work on Andrea's accounts, reporting to me but also helping her directly. And when I get that finalized, I plan to move back to LA and resume my job with the police department. If you're with me, we'll both move back. How does that sound?"

"Feasible, but—"

"More than feasible," he interrupted. "Permanent. Us." He got down on one knee then. "I don't have a ring yet, but I'll ask anyway. Harper Morsley, will you marry me?"

Harper was astounded. Thrilled.

He loved her too? He wanted to marry her? To work out a life together starting here, but one where they'd move back to LA, where it would be easier for her to work on her research, contact her editors, continue her writing career? Maybe even accept Sally's offer to become an editor and do it remotely.

With Bryson by her side?

"Oh, yes, Bryson." She pulled his hands so he soon stood in front of her. "I'll marry you. And maybe I can even write some wonderful, salable articles about engagements, weddings and happily-ever-afters, including dogs in the stories."

He laughed as he looked down at her. And then they kissed.

Oh, yes, she looked forward to their H-E-A. And to be with Bryson, forevermore.

What a tale to tell!

* * * * *

*Look for more books in Linda O. Johnston's
miniseries, Shelter of Secrets,
coming soon, wherever
Harlequin Romantic Suspense
books are sold!*

HARLEQUIN
Reader Service

Enjoyed your book?

Try the perfect subscription for Romance readers and get more great books like this delivered right to your door.

See why over 10+ million readers have tried Harlequin Reader Service.

Start with a Free Welcome Collection with free books and a gift—valued over $20.

Choose any series in print or ebook. See website for details and order today:

TryReaderService.com/subscriptions

RSBPA24R